Wildwitch
Oblivion

Wildwitch

Oblivion

Lene Kaaberbøl

Illustrated by Rohan Eason

Translated by Charlotte Barslund

PUSHKIN CHILDREN'S BOOKS

Pushkin Press
71–75 Shelton Street
London, WC2H 9JQ

Original text copyright © Lene Kaaberbøl, Copenhagen 2011

Published by agreement with
Copenhagen Literary Agency, Copenhagen

Translation © Charlotte Barslund, 2016

Illustrations © Rohan Eason

Wildwitch: Oblivion was originally published in Danish
as *Vildheks: Viridians Blod* by Alvilda in 2011

This translation first published by
Pushkin Children's Books in 2016

3 5 7 9 8 6 4 2

ISBN 978 1 782690 84 9

Set in Berling Nova by Tetragon, London
Printed and bound by CPI Group (UK) Ltd, Croydon CR0 4YY

www.pushkinpress.com

CONTENTS

1   The Kestrel   7
2   Shanaia   14
3   Air Raid   19
4   Aunt Isa   25
5   Shanaia's Story   32
6   Remember Viridian   43
7   Being Walked All Over   50
8   It Gets Worse   58
9   Bad Dreams   64
10 Missing   69
11 The Empty House   75
12 Wild Dogs   80
13 Lop-Ear   87
14 Westmark   93
15 The Nothing   102
16 The Sisters   111
17 Chimera's Voice   118
18 Guard Dog   130
19 The Blank Book   140
20 Oblivion   148

21	The Wheel	154
22	"No man, no woman, no child."	160
23	Blood Arts	164
24	Life Stealer	171
25	Something Is Better Than Nothing	179
26	Excuses	192
27	Cat Smiles	201

CHAPTER ONE

The Kestrel

"Do you like it?" my dad asked, watching me closely.

"Oh, I do," I lied. "It's perfect."

The room was bigger than my room at home with my mum on Mercury Street; the walls were glaringly white and still smelt of fresh paint. The end wall was entirely glass, with a glass door leading to a balcony and, if I looked hard, I could make out a tiny stretch of actual water on the other side of all the warehouses, containers and dockside cranes. My stuff from his old house had been packed into a couple of orange removal crates, now sitting on the new bed he had bought for me.

My dad had got a new job. Instead of living at the other end of the country in an old terraced house with whitewashed walls, a tiled roof and a garden full of apple trees and badly kept lawn, he had moved here – into a brand-new, undoubtedly wildly expensive flat in the new harbour development, only fifteen minutes from Mercury Street on the number 18 bus. And he said he couldn't wait to spend more time with me than before.

"Before", the last seven years of my life, that is, we'd had a fixed routine: a fortnight in the summer holidays, one week over Christmas, half my Easter holidays and two weekends in the autumn. Last autumn, we had managed just the one weekend because of the events with Chimera and the cat and Aunt Isa, who had had to teach me what she referred to as *Self-defence for wildwitches, lesson one.* Events about which, incidentally, my dad knew absolutely nothing. He believed, as did most people, that I'd been ill for a few weeks with Cat Scratch Disease.

Apart from that little hiccough, we'd stuck to our routine – lovely holidays in his old house where I would play with Mick and Sarah from next door, and Dad would take time off so we could go to the local swimming pool, bake clumsy bread rolls, play Yahtzee, make popcorn and watch a lot of old movies together. He was really, really good at being Holiday Dad.

Now he was Holiday Dad no more. He had sold the terraced house on Chestnut Street, which meant no more hanging out with Mick and Sarah, no more building dens among the redcurrant bushes, no more hot chocolate in front of the fire during thunderstorms when the rain pelted the roof tiles and splashed down onto the patio in the spot where the gutter always overflowed.

He was thrilled that we would be so much closer, and I was too. I could see the upside of being able to pop over during the week, rather than having months pass between my visits. Except that it felt a bit as if someone had sold my holiday home without checking with me first.

"You get the evening sun on the balcony," he said, and opened the glass door. "We can sit outside and barbecue in the summer."

It was February and freezing cold. I managed to curb my enthusiasm for a barbecue.

An icy wind rattled the new blinds violently and a smell of diesel, tar and brine blew into the room. Then, without warning, a feathery missile swooped down the front of the building, continued right across the balcony and shot directly through the open door.

"What...?" my dad exclaimed.

It was a bird of prey, not a very big one actually, but between the white walls of my room it seemed enormous. Fanning its tail feathers, pale apart from their black tips, it braked sharply, froze in mid-flap for a split second, then made directly for me. I instinctively held out my arm and it landed a little clumsily on my wrist. Its yellow talons contracted and went through the sleeve of my jumper and into my skin, but even so the bird had to keep flapping its dappled wings to stay upright.

The reason it was wobbling was that it was holding something in one talon. A piece of folded paper, which it extended towards me in a decidedly bossy manner. It emitted a couple of imperious chirp-chirp sounds, and I took the note from it because that was quite clearly what it wanted me to do. The instant I'd obeyed its command, it took wing once more and streaked through the balcony door and into the sky beyond.

"But..." my dad stood with his mouth hanging open, staring after it. "But that was a kestrel!"

I quickly stuffed the note into the pocket of my jeans while his attention was on the bird.

"You see more and more of them in the city these days," I said casually, trying to make it sound as if kestrels flew into people's living rooms on a daily basis.

"Eh... right, but... it must have been a tame one, surely? Was it wearing jesses?"

"It might have been," I said. "I didn't really have time to see." I was fairly sure it was a wild bird that had never been tamed, trained or restrained with jesses, but I decided not to mention that.

"How remarkable," my dad said. "There would appear to be more wildlife in the city than I had expected." Then he noticed my hand.

"Oh, no, Clara," he said. "It scratched you."

I looked down. He was right. A tiny trickle of blood ran down my palm, from a single deep scratch on my wrist. It wasn't much and yet a strange, cold feeling stirred in my tummy. I couldn't help thinking that this was how it had all begun last autumn – with a wild animal, four scratches and a few drops of warm, red blood on a rainy morning when I was supposed to be on my way to school. I could remember only too vividly the weight of the cat body and the sensation of its moist, rough tongue licking up the blood.

That was how Cat and I met. Now he lived with us on Mercury Street, but anyone mistaking him for a pet would be sorely misguided. Although he had fitted himself comfortably into my routines, he never neglected an opportunity to tell me who owned whom – you can guess for yourself what his view was – and he still went his own ways. Unless he was lying next to me, purring, I rarely knew where he was.

We had told the neighbours that he was a special Norwegian Forest cat to explain away his unusually generous size.

"You'd better clean that up," my dad said. "Did you have a tetanus injection back when that cat scratched you?"

"Yes," I said, and marched dutifully to the guest bathroom and stuck my wrist under the cold tap. I caught a glimpse of myself in the mirror and leaned closer to the sink. The four small, vertical scars that Cat's claws had left were normally just thin, white lines I hardly noticed. Now I suddenly thought they looked more prominent.

"Are you allowed to keep cats here?" I asked.

Dad hesitated. "Not really," he then said. "But if you want – what did you say his name was? Is it just Cat?"

"Yes," I said, well aware that it wasn't very imaginative, but it was the only word that suited his wilful nature and large, black, furry, feline body.

"If you want to bring him when you visit, you'll need a carry cage and a litter tray for him, and as long as you keep him in the flat, then I guess it should be OK."

Cat in a cage? Not in a month of Sundays, I thought. I wasn't dumb enough to even suggest it.

The scratch soon stopped bleeding. The kestrel had tried its best not to hurt me or I would have had deep holes from all four talons, but it must have been hard to avoid damage completely when landing on one leg.

"Does it hurt?"

"No," I said. "It's nothing."

"I'll make some hot chocolate," Dad said. "Meanwhile you can unpack your things. Make yourself more at home..."

I knew he could tell that I didn't like my new room quite as much as I claimed. He was no fool. At least, not often. He put his hand on my head and ruffled my hair.

"Everything will be all right," he said.

I waited until I could hear him potter about in the shiny new white kitchen. Then I took the note out of my pocket and unfolded it.

FAIRYDELL PARK it said in capital letters. *Tomorrow. One hour before sunset, the north path, third bench from the gate.* And at the bottom, a tiny animal head supposed to be a ferret's.

It wasn't, as I'd presumed, from Aunt Isa. It had to be from a wildwitch – who else would use a wild kestrel like some kind of carrier pigeon? – and I knew only one person whose wildfriend was a ferret.

Why did Shanaia want to meet up with me? She wasn't someone who enjoyed girly chats and hugs. It had to be important.

CHAPTER 2

Shanaia

"She's supposed to be here. Or hereabouts," I said, double-checking the by now rather crumpled note. I could still see the marks where the kestrel had clutched it in its talons. *One hour before sunset, the north path, third bench from the gate.*

"Perhaps we're too early," said Oscar, who had stopped so that Woofer could pee against a barberry bush. "Or too late. Why couldn't she just write a quarter past five like normal people? If that's what she meant...?"

"Because she's a wildwitch," I said. "As far as she's concerned, it's all about natural time, not minutes on some watch." But even I had to admit that it had been a pain to find out what time the sun set in early February.

Fairydell Park couldn't be less magical if it tried. It was squashed between the railway, an old meat packing plant and a strip of rather neglected-looking allotment gardens. In the summer, it might boast a few leafy trees and the odd intrepid sunbather. In winter it was merely muddy, gloomy and desolate. The paths and the soggy grass were littered with burger wrappers and pizza boxes and empty beer cans, and though it seemed a street cleaner had made a half-hearted attempt to pick up some of the litter and bag it in black bin liners, it made little difference since the bags had simply been dumped behind the benches.

"There's nobody here," Oscar said. "Please can we go home?"

"You're the one who insisted on coming with me," I said. "You were the one dead set on meeting a *real* wildwitch."

"Yes, because I thought it would be super cool. But there aren't any wildwitches, are there? Apart from you, I mean."

"And I don't count, of course..."

"Oh, stop it. You know what I mean."

I counted the benches again to make sure I had the right one – third from the gate. I did, but it remained stubbornly vacant. I don't know if I'd expected Shanaia to materialize out of the grey February air just because I had turned my back for a moment, but she certainly hadn't.

"Let's do one more round," I said. "Just to be on the safe side."

"Clara, there are people with vegetable patches bigger than this park. She's not here!"

One of the bin liners stirred. My heart jumped into my throat and I let out a startled squeak.

"What's wrong?" Oscar said.

I pointed. "There," I said. "It *moved*..."

The plastic fluttered in the wind, but that wasn't it. And now Oscar could see it too. A pointy, white head stuck out of the rubbish, a head with round, dark ears, blood-red eyes and whiskers longer than the width of its head.

"It's one of those... thingamajigs," he said. "Like weasels."

"A ferret," I said, and felt the February chill spread inside me. "It's Shanaia's..."

I squatted down on my haunches next to the bench and carefully extended my hand towards the ferret. It widened its jaw and hissed at me so I could see all its needle-sharp teeth. It wasn't until then that I realized that the pile of rubbish wasn't *all* rubbish. Under the cover of the black bags, I could see a shoulder sticking out of a torn leather jacket. That bit of denim among the milk cartons, pizza boxes and popcorn bags wasn't just a pair of old jeans someone had thrown away. It had a leg inside it. And now I saw a hand, a hand with pale fingertips and long, silver-painted nails protruding from a pair of cut-off black leather gloves with studs across the knuckles.

It was Shanaia.

"Is... is she dead?" Oscar asked. Woofer whined anxiously, then barked at the ferret and possibly also at Shanaia. Earlier he had wandered past the bench – twice – without taking any notice of the bin bags at all.

"Go away," I ordered the ferret sternly. "We're only trying to help her."

Perhaps I had become enough of a wildwitch for it to understand. At any rate, it graciously refrained from sinking its teeth into my hand as I started tossing rubbish and plastic aside so I could get a better look at Shanaia.

She was breathing.

Her eyes were closed and her face was as cold as ice, but she was breathing.

"She's not dead," I exclaimed with relief.

But what had happened to her?

CHAPTER 3

Air Raid

"Shouldn't we call an ambulance?" Oscar said.

"I'm not sure that's such a good idea," I replied. "What about the ferret? There's no way it'll be allowed inside a hospital. I think we'd better call Aunt Isa."

"But she doesn't have a phone," Oscar objected.

Actually, she did. Last autumn I'd convinced her to buy a mobile, but she lived so far off the grid that she could use it only if she climbed the hill behind her farmhouse. She could call me, but I couldn't call her – not unless she just happened to have trudged up to the top of the ridge to admire the view.

Even so I gave it a try. Crackle, crackle. "We're currently unable to connect you to the number you have called..." What a surprise.

I touched Shanaia's cheek again. She was still ice-cold and showed no signs of coming to.

"Eh..." Oscar said. "Clara... it's getting darker, don't you think? And... foggier?"

I looked up. He was right. The sky was leaden, black almost, and thin, grey fingers of fog were creeping towards us across the muddy grass. There was nothing unusual about the sky darkening less than half an hour before sunset, but those weaving, grey tentacles... It was almost as if they were searching for something. One of them wound itself around Oscar's ankle, and he instinctively lifted his leg.

"Gross..." he exclaimed.

The black sky suddenly cracked with a hollow boom and ejected a wedge of white. My jaw dropped as I stared at the whiteness hurtling towards us like a nose-diving jet plane. Within seconds, we were surrounded by a blizzard of huge, white birds.

"What...?" Oscar began, but before he'd finished his question, the first bird had crashed into his chest and sent him reeling. The air was filled with screaming, flapping, pecking seagulls with red eyes and yellow, red-stained beaks. At first Woofer let out a couple of aggressive barks, then he howled pitifully and attempted to make his escape. The yank on the leash jerked Oscar completely off his feet, and the seagulls pounced on him as if he were a pile of especially delicious kitchen scraps on the top of a skip.

They didn't touch me. Only Oscar, Woofer and Shanaia.

"Go away!" I yelled at them, waving my arms around. "Back off! *NOW GO AWAY!*" It was the only wildwitchery I had ever been any good at, making animals – and some people – go away when I shouted at them.

Only this time it didn't work. Or maybe it did, they kept away from me. But not from the others. I grabbed a flapping white wing and pulled a giant herring gull off Oscar. Woofer howled and yelped and tried to get away, but couldn't because his leash was still wrapped around Oscar's wrist. Slam – slam – peck, slam – peck – peck, one after the other, the seagulls pounded them like feathered bombs with their long, hard beaks, and Oscar was yelling and shouting and rolling around, flailing his arms to try and keep them off him.

"*CAT!*" I shouted. "Cat, help!!"

I had no idea where he was or if he could hear me; all I knew was that I couldn't handle this alone. I tore at the pecking seagulls, yanking them off Oscar, Woofer and Shanaia with panicking hands, grabbing greasy white wings, stumpy tails, knobbly, yellow legs, I didn't care what, all that mattered was to get them *off*.

"*CAT!*" I yelled again, louder this time. "*HELP!*"

And suddenly I was no longer alone. No longer the only one fighting the seagulls. Blackbirds, sparrows, bullfinches with beaks like secateurs, two ginger urban foxes, four feral tabbies hissing and snarling, a black and white flock of magpies, a heron with a massive wingspan and a neck like some prehistoric flying reptile... More animals joined me, rooks, crows, even a couple of mallards and a dozen brown rats, a flapping, snapping, biting, heaving army erupting from the earth and the sky, the bushes and the trees. And Cat. Cat was here too.

Grrrrrrrrrrrrrrrrrrrrrrrrrrr. He struck the mob of seagulls like a black torpedo, as big as a panther and with claws like fishhooks. *Back off, birdbrains! She's mine!* I could hear his thoughts much more clearly than Oscar's incoherent shouting.

The seagulls retreated. Many had been injured, blood stained their white feathers red and one of them was dragging its entrails and two broken wings behind it in the gravel. They looked like normal seagulls now, with normal pale yellow eyes, and those who could, flew off. Cat snapped the neck of the eviscerated gull with a single violent swipe from his paw, and one of the foxes ran off with another feathered and bloody bundle in its jaws. The magpies pursued a weakened, barely airborne tern through the leafless bushes and I think they caught it somewhere behind the rhododendrons.

Cat sniffed the dead seagull on the path. I was more worried about Oscar, who was sitting up slowly, but definitely didn't look his best. His baseball cap had come off and his hair, quite upright and tufty at the best of times, was a mess of reddish clumps. Blood trickled from his nose and from one eyebrow, and all of his face and both his hands were covered in scratches. It was just as well that it was February and he had been wearing winter clothing – his puffer jacket had suffered multiple tears from which man-made fibres stuck out, but it had undoubtedly protected him against a lot of the pecking and scratching.

"Ouch," he winced. "That really hurt. Stupid, sodding seagulls!"

I took it as a good sign that he could still swear. Woofer licked Oscar's cheek and looked somewhat contrite and defeated.

Oscar touched his nose gingerly.

"What is *up* with those seagulls?" he wanted to know. "Was it more of that wildwitch stuff?"

Though he was the one who was bleeding, he didn't seem nearly as shaken as I was. Perhaps he didn't understand just how close he'd come to being pecked to death. I could never have managed to fight off the seagulls on my own; I'd only succeeded because I'd had help.

"Was that Chimera?" I asked Cat. "Did she make the seagulls attack us?" I knew they would never have done so of their own accord.

Cat merely hissed and bared the claws on one of his black front paws. He didn't know who was behind it, but if he ever found out, then the sneaky little rat had better watch out.

Oscar got up.

"So now what?" he said. "Are you sure we shouldn't call an ambulance?"

Cat arched his back, then stretched. *Isa*, he said. *You need Isa*.

I couldn't agree more. Only I didn't know how to get hold of her, did I?

At that very moment my mobile rang.

CHAPTER 4

Aunt Isa

She came walking through the fog with Hoot-Hoot on her shoulder and Star following at her heels like a large dog rather than the sturdy, round-backed, woolly pony she was. Hoot-Hoot spread his broad wings and stared at us with round owl eyes. Oscar whispered: "Awesome!" And then appeared to lose the power of speech.

He had my sympathy. I was used to seeing Aunt Isa at home where she belonged, in the small stone farmhouse in the middle of the woods, with paraffin lamps and a log burner and hibernating hedgehogs in shoeboxes in the living room. She didn't look exactly ordinary there either, but still... less out of place.

Emerging from the dense, grey fog, in her broad-brimmed hat and long plaits, an owl perched on her shoulder and a horse with no bridle or saddle trotting behind her – right here in Fairydell Park with its tarmac paths, empty cola cans and council park benches, and the traffic roaring past on Fairydell Road... Well, my aunt Isa looked exactly what she was: a witch. A wildwitch who could travel the wildways and appear any place any time, a creature from a world where you didn't change buses or drive cars to get from A to B, and because she was angry, she also looked fierce. She really looked as if she could turn someone into a frog if they didn't behave – and if she didn't think it would be a rotten thing to do to all the other ordinary decent real frogs.

She didn't say a word; just nodded briefly to me and dropped to her knees by Shanaia's side. She

put a hand on her neck, right below the ear, and began to sing. The wildsong wound itself around us almost like the fog tentacles had done, low and high at the same time, a sudden warmth, a scent of soil and wet leaves, a quiver of life deep in our bones.

Shanaia coughed lightly and I saw a trickle from the corner of her mouth, something slimy and pink that didn't look healthy. She coughed again, more violently this time, and the ferret twitched and then made a wild, jubilant jump for joy. It gave a happy sort of whine and rubbed itself against Aunt Isa's hand as if it were a cuddly kitten, and Shanaia opened her eyes.

She hadn't recovered full consciousness. Her gaze was blurry and confused, and she was unable to sit up without help. One fist clenched a tuft of greasy grass and she began to shake all over.

"Shanaia," Aunt Isa called out. "Shanaia, we're here. You're here. Come back to us."

What did she mean by that?

"Shanaia!" Loud and commanding. Shanaia's whole body suddenly jerked and something in her eyes changed.

"Yes," she said in a croaky and very quiet voice. "I'm here now." As if she really hadn't been, before. Then she coughed lightly again and closed her eyes.

"Help me get her up on Star," Aunt Isa said. "She can't walk on her own."

Shanaia's skin was still cold, but not as icy as before. She tried to stand, but she had almost no strength left and getting her onto Star's broad, round back was a struggle.

"Hang on to the mane," Aunt Isa said to her. "We'll take care of everything else."

"Yes," Shanaia whispered, flopping forward onto Star's neck. She grabbed the coarse, bristly mane with both hands, but I had to support her from one side and Oscar from the other to make sure she stayed on. The ferret popped its head out from under the collar of her leather jacket and emitted a string of tiny, high-pitched eeek-eeek-eeek noises that sounded anxious and aggressive at the same time.

"You have to help," Aunt Isa said, her voice straining with the effort. "Both of you. We need to get her back to my house."

"But..." Oscar began.

"I'll take you home afterwards," Aunt Isa said. Woofer just gazed up at Aunt Isa with total adoration and wagged his tail so his broad backside swung from side to side. "Clara, call your mum and tell her I'll bring you back as soon as I can."

I don't think Aunt Isa had any idea just how my mum would react to such a message, so I decided to text her instead: *Oscar and I are with Aunt Isa. Please would you call Dad? Will explain later.* Right now it was easier.

"Is this the wildways?" Oscar whispered to me as we started walking.

"Not yet," I said.

Aunt Isa led the way and Star followed very carefully as if she were scared of dropping Shanaia. The fog grew denser, and the noise from the traffic on Fairydell Road disappeared.

"*Now* we're on the wildways," I said to Oscar.

When we emerged from the wildways fog near Aunt Isa's farmhouse, it had grown completely dark. A huge and nearly full moon hung right above the treetops and a fine sprinkling of snow and hoar frost on the meadow and the gravel track turned everything blue. The meadow, the track, the thatched roofs on the farmhouse and the barn, the apple trees in the orchard... everything glistened frostily blue in the moonlight. The fire must still be going in the wood burner because a fine blue trickle of smoke rose from the chimney. Star whinnied loudly, and from inside the house we could hear Bumble bark with excitement, which made Woofer go completely hyper, pulling and straining at his leash like a mad dog.

Aunt Isa helped Shanaia down from the pony.

"Please would you see to Star?" she asked me.

"Of course," I said, although the barn was frankly not where I wanted to be right now. Shanaia was still barely conscious and had told us nothing about what happened, and my curiosity was nearly killing me. But Star deserved a good feed and lots of cuddles and a good rub down, given how sweet and cautious she had been, so careful not to drop her weakened rider.

Oscar was standing in the middle of the farmyard, looking around him with widening eyes. I don't think it was the farmyard in itself or the thatched roof or the grey stone walls. Rather, it was the fact that we were here, quite clearly deep in the forest, when only ten minutes ago we had been in Fairydell Park with the traffic zooming past just on the other side of the fence.

"Wow..." he said. "What happened?"

"The wildways," I said. "I told you."

"Yes. But..."

But being here was completely different from my telling him about it. I did understand that.

"You'll get used to it," I said, although I wasn't entirely sure I was used to it myself.

Oscar helped me with Star. He had little experience with horses, but I showed him how to brush her, first in soft circles with the plastic curry comb, then with the dandy brush in long strokes in the direction of her coat. We stood either side of her, rubbing and brushing until she dropped her lower lip and looked blissful, and actually it felt really pleasant and quiet and safe after everything that had happened. We let Woofer off his leash and he cautiously greeted the bravest of the goats. The goat promptly butted him playfully with its small, stumpy horns, making Woofer yelp with fright and seek cover behind Oscar. Woofer wasn't quite the sort of action dog hero that scaled walls, disarmed bad guys, and jumped into harbours to save his drowning master. To be honest, he was a bit of a couch potato. But he was a very sweet dog all the same.

Cat had disappeared, and I took this to be a good sign. Had he believed I was still in danger, I'm sure he would have stayed with me.

"What do you think is wrong with Shanaia?" Oscar asked.

"I don't know," I said. "But if you'll help me give Star some hay and fresh water, then we can go inside and find out."

CHAPTER 5

Shanaia's Story

There was a crackling fire in the log burner, and Bumble had put his head – along with about half of the rest of his body – across my lap. He was so heavy that my legs were starting to go numb, but I didn't push him away because his presence was so warm and reassuring. Woofer had curled up at Oscar's feet and was snoring loudly.

All very nice and cosy – but there was nothing cosy and certainly nothing nice about what had happened to Shanaia.

"When Westmark was taken from me," Shanaia began, "people tried to make me feel better by saying there were lots of other nice places to live. They just didn't get it. I was born there. But more than that. I *belong* there in a way I can't explain. Something inside me is... is anchored there. Like a limpet to a rock. I can travel, I can visit other places – but I can't *live* anywhere else. Do you understand?"

She looked so pale and weak that I just nodded even though I didn't know exactly what she meant. Was she describing a kind of homesickness? I knew what it was like to be homesick. I would often miss Mercury Street when I visited Aunt Isa and sometimes also my dad and the house in Chestnut Street.

Though that was now a thing of the past. I remembered the pang I had felt when Dad told me he'd sold up and was moving. Perhaps what Shanaia was feeling was a bit like that? Only much worse?

"I was so young when my parents died that I don't really remember them. But I remember Westmark."

It was news to me that Shanaia was an orphan, though I did know that Chimera had somehow taken her childhood home from her. To lose both your parents and your home... I felt a stab of sympathy.

"There's something unusual about your life cord," Aunt Isa announced. "It doesn't just connect you to all living things, like other people's. It seems to have an extra root."

Shanaia nodded. "That's Westmark. You do understand!" Her tense features softened, and her hand, which had been restlessly waving while she struggled to explain, now sank onto the patchwork quilt and settled there.

I studied Shanaia closely, but could see nothing except a deathly pale and exhausted young wild-witch with far too many cuts and bruises. I realized I had a very long way to go before I became even half as skilled as Aunt Isa.

"So when the Raven Mothers exiled Chimera, Westmark was all I could think about. Finally the Raven Mothers would have to take it from her and return it to me. Or so I thought."

"But surely that's what they did?" I said. I seemed to remember Aunt Isa writing something to that effect in her Christmas card to me.

"Yes and no. They gave me back the deeds to Westmark, but they wouldn't help me make Chimera leave."

"Many ravens died," Aunt Isa said. "It'll be years before the Raven Mothers regain their former strength."

"Yes. They said that I had to wait. But... I couldn't." She fumbled for her leather jacket which hung over the back of the sofa where she was lying. Then she handed me a worn leather wallet. "Look."

I took the wallet without quite understanding why she was giving it to me. It contained no money or credit cards or anything like that. It was completely empty, apart from a dog-eared photograph in the plastic pocket where most grown-ups keep a photograph of their children, or their husband or wife. But there were no people in Shanaia's picture. Only a narrow beach washed by the placid waves of a sheltered bay, and some tall, craggy cliffs topped with grass. In the distance, I could make out the contours of an old house with lots of chimneys perched on the edge of the cliffs. Somehow it looked like the house at the end of the world as it clung there, on the verge of tumbling into the deep. A huge flock of seagulls floated on sharp, white wings in the up-draught. I was immediately reminded of the incident in the park and had to repress a shiver.

I felt I ought to say something nice about the place, given how much it meant to Shanaia, but for now I couldn't get the seagulls' beaks and their red eyes out of my mind. I gave her back the wallet without saying a word.

Oscar looked at her and then at me, and tried to fathom the exchange.

"Why are the ravens so important?" he then asked. "The dead ones, I mean?"

"Without them, the Raven Mothers can't see," Aunt Isa said. "And it's difficult to fight if you're blind."

"So what did you do?" he asked Shanaia. "Did you gather an army?"

She stared at him with a frown. "An army?"

"Yes. So that you could take back your castle."

"Westmark isn't a castle," she said. "It's just... a place. And what would I do with an army?"

"Aren't you meant to defeat this Chimera and all her deadly hordes?"

Shanaia gave me a what-is-he-on-about sort of look.

"It's not quite like a computer game," I said gently. "I don't believe Chimera has any hordes. And Shanaia definitely doesn't have an army."

"It might have made a difference if I had," Shanaia said. "Because Chimera does actually have hordes of a kind now."

"What do you mean?" Aunt Isa said sharply. "Don't tell me any wildwitches have sided with her? After all, she's an outlaw."

"No, no wildwitches," Shanaia said. "But she has done something to the animals of Westmark. They... they're not free any more."

"Are you talking about soul-stripped animals?" Aunt Isa's voice was so outraged that Bumble lifted his head. "Has she enslaved them?"

"What's that?" Oscar asked.

"A heinous crime," Aunt Isa replied darkly. "To take away an animal's free will... not to call it or ask it to be quiet while you help it, but to overpower and enslave it... that's unworthy of any wildwitch.

I'm aware that Chimera has flouted her wildwitch oath many times, but that she would be so brazen... I never would have believed that."

"The seagulls," I said. "And the bats last year..."

"What are you talking about, Clara?"

I told her about the bats that had caused me to fall from the rope ladder during the wildfire trial and the court case against Chimera, and about the seagulls in Fairydell Park.

"Could they really have come all the way from Westmark?" I asked.

"Perhaps," Shanaia said. "If she sent them by the wildways." She looked at Oscar's scratches and bruises and then at me. "But they didn't attack you?" she then said.

"Not really. You and Oscar bore the brunt of it. And poor Woofer."

Woofer's tail drowsily bashed the floor a couple of times, then he went back to sleep.

Aunt Isa nodded slowly.

"That sounds like soul-stripping."

Shanaia heaved a deep sigh.

"My plan was just to have a look and get some idea of how difficult it would be to make her leave, if she refused to go voluntarily. But I'd been there less than an hour when they found me. First the birds. Then a pack of wild dogs. Or rather – a pack of soul-stripped dogs. They surrounded me and Elfrida..." She stroked the ferret across its back with one hand. "...and I couldn't get away from them. Then Chimera herself turned up."

At that moment Shanaia's face lost all expression, but I don't think it was because she didn't feel anything. Quite the opposite.

"She bound me with cold iron," she said in a monotone voice. "And there was nothing I could do about it. And then she started to... to question me."

Something in Aunt Isa's face contorted and I didn't need to ask any more questions to know that the interrogation had been both painful and humiliating. Shanaia wouldn't even look at us now.

"What did she want to know?" Aunt Isa asked her gently.

"Lots of stuff about Westmark. And about Clara."

"About Clara? What specifically?"

"What she could do. I mean, as a wildwitch."

Not much, I thought glumly.

"About who her parents were. And something about cold iron," Shanaia went on.

"She bound me with iron too," I said, and couldn't help touching my neck. I hadn't forgotten the cold, sharp pressure of the iron collar.

"But you could still use your powers," Aunt Isa said. "You made her go away. I'm sure she's mystified by that. Did she say anything else?"

"No."

Suddenly Cat leapt up on the sofa to Shanaia. I hadn't even noticed him coming inside with us. He pushed his nose so close to Shanaia's face that the ferret hissed at him, and Cat made a noise somewhere between a purr and a growl. Shanaia blinked.

"Wait," she whispered. "Yes... There was more. Something about... I think it was Vidian, or something like that."

The latter made me sit up with a jerk.

"Viridian? Could she have said Viridian?"

"Yes."

"Who is that?" I asked.

"I don't know," Shanaia said wearily. She sounded as if she didn't think it mattered very much. "I've never heard about it. Or her. Or him."

But I had. Twice.

"When I first met Chimera," I said. "And the second time was when she put the iron collar on me and I made her go away. She said something to me: 'Blood of Viridian.'" Yes, those had been her words. And she had glared at me as if it had something to do with me somehow.

"I'll go heat up some soup," Aunt Isa said, almost as if she hadn't heard me.

"Soup?" I was baffled. How could she not think that stuff about Viridian was important?

"Shanaia needs to get something warm inside her," she said. "And I imagine the rest of you are hungry as well?"

There it was again, the purring growl. Cat's tail swished slowly from side to side as if he'd seen another tomcat or some potential prey. Or... did he actually have the nerve to growl at *Aunt Isa*?

"Cat," I warned him. "Behave yourself."

He stopped growling. Instead he jumped up on the armrest of the easy chair and stared Bumble down until Bumble capitulated and shifted himself to the floor. Cat curled up on my lap and sent a yellow-glared, bristly thought through my head. *Mine.*

"Settle down," I said, stroking his back. "Nobody's trying to take me away from you."

But perhaps I spoke too soon.

"Clara." Shanaia looked at me with a strangely intense gaze. "You have to help me. You're the only one who can."

"Me??"

"Yes. That's why I sent the kestrel."

"But... Why do you want my help?"

"To get Westmark back."

"But I can't do that!" The mere thought of approaching Chimera of my own free will… "What makes you think I can?"

"Because cold iron doesn't hold you. Because the soul-stripped animals can't hurt you. But most of all… because Chimera is afraid of you."

"What?!" Shanaia wasn't well, I told myself. She didn't know what she was saying. It was possibly the most far-fetched claim I'd ever heard. Chimera would have me for breakfast – without even breaking a sweat. Her greatest difficulty would be to decide whether to eat me roasted or raw. The notion that she was in any way afraid of me… No. Impossible. Absurd. Ridiculous.

"You have to!" Shanaia said hoarsely and grabbed the hem of my skirt, which was the only part of me she could reach. "No one else can. Or wants to."

I stared down at her white fingers clutching the coarse denim.

"You can't be serious," I whispered.

"Clara still has much to learn," Aunt Isa interjected. "I believe Chimera is too dangerous for her…"

You could say that again.

"I really can't," I said, trying to ignore the desperate hand and Cat's burning gaze, which for some

41

reason was aimed at me right now. "I'm really sorry for you, for Westmark, but... no."

Shanaia's fingers slowly released their grip and her hand flopped onto the floor as if she no longer had the strength to lift it.

"Then there is no one," she whispered, and closed her eyes.

Oscar sent me a strange look, reproachful, I thought. And I felt like a tiny, cowardly louse. But what choice did I have? There was absolutely nothing I could do against someone like Chimera. Nothing at all.

CHAPTER 6

Remember Viridian

Although it was nearly one o'clock in the morning, the light was still on in the flat in Mercury Street.

"Aren't you going to come upstairs with me?" I asked Aunt Isa, trying not to sound too desperate. Only it would be so much easier if she would explain everything to my mum.

She glanced at me sideways.

"I think I'd better," she said. "But I can't stay long. Shanaia needs me."

Hoot-Hoot took off from her shoulder with a silent beat of his broad wings, and disappeared into the darkness above the street lamps. The mice in Mercury Street had better watch out tonight.

Without Hoot-Hoot Aunt Isa looked a tad more normal. Still, it was probably just as well that most of our neighbours had gone to bed.

The light came on in the stairwell a split second before my fingers touched the switch. I looked up and wasn't at all surprised to see Mum in the doorway to our flat. She has always had a way of knowing if it was me coming home. It occurred to me that she might have a kind of wildsense where I was concerned – a bit like the way an animal always knows where its young are. She didn't say anything; she just disappeared back into the flat and left the door open so that we could follow. It wasn't until we were all inside – including Oscar and Woofer – that she launched her attack. Not on me, at least not yet, but on her older sister.

"Who do you think you are?" she hissed through clenched teeth.

"Milla..." Aunt Isa began and made a reassuring gesture. But my mum wasn't in a mood to be placated.

"No. Don't you *dare* shush me. Just what gives you the right to march into my life – into Clara's life – and take her as if she were yours? Without asking. Without calling me. Without... me. You simply can't do that!"

"I did send you a text..." I piped up.

Mum shot me a single, furious glare which promised that she would get to me later. Then she turned her attention back on Aunt Isa.

"I had to lie to Clara's dad. And Oscar's mum. You forced me to do that."

"I'm sorry if..."

"But that's not the worst. The worst is..." Now she looked at me again, but with a completely different expression that struck right at my core. Not angry. Desperate. And then she seemed to lose the power of speech. No more words came out, only a tiny, strangled sound. And I could see that she was on the verge of tears.

"I wouldn't have done it if it hadn't been important," Isa said quietly. "If there had been any other way. But there wasn't."

"Isa *helped* us," I said. "Mum, it's OK. And we're all safely back now."

Oscar cleared his throat.

"Ahem... me and Woofer should probably be..."

My mum shook her head. "No. You'll be sleeping here tonight. That's what I've arranged with your mum. She doesn't know that you... that you've been away. I had no idea how to explain to her that Clara's aunt Isa is..." She ran out of words again, and this time I had a better idea of why. I, too, would struggle to explain to Oscar's tough lawyer mum that my aunt was a wildwitch who could talk to the animals and travel the wildways so that a distance of several hundred kilometres meant hardly anything at all.

"Probably for the best," Oscar interjected quickly.

My mum shook her head. "There's nothing 'best' about it," she said. "And you don't have to lie to your mum to protect us. I just didn't know how to make her believe that..."

"No," Oscar said. "She's not really into all that supernatural stuff. She gets really worked up about people believing in horoscopes even."

"I have to go," Isa said. "But Milla... the children haven't done anything wrong. On the contrary. They acted with strength, courage and intelligence. Is that so terrible?"

My face went all red. I didn't feel strong, courageous or intelligent. Especially not courageous, given I had just said no to helping Shanaia.

Mum looked at Aunt Isa.

"Your job was to teach her to survive," she said. "That was all. You were *not* to... to expose her to danger again. Take her from me again. Turn her into... into something completely different from what she is."

Aunt Isa shook her head. "I'm not turning her into anything," she said. "I'm not the one who decides who Clara will be. And Milla... neither are you."

"Go away," my mum said, her voice sagging with tiredness. "Go away, and leave Clara alone."

I had been expecting a massive telling off when Aunt Isa had left. But Mum said hardly anything at all. She just fetched some extra bedlinen, so that Oscar and Woofer could sleep on the floor in my room, and she even asked if we were hungry. Oscar had a bowl of cornflakes, but I couldn't get a thing down, though my tummy was rumbling. I hated it when Mum was sad. It ate away at me, and I would always try to make her happy again as fast as I could. But this time I didn't know how.

I was dog-tired when my alarm clock went off the next morning. It's an old-fashioned one, neither digital nor electric. It has to be wound up every day, and it sounds like a fire alarm when it goes off. But it has black Mickey Mouse ears, nose and eyes, and I've had it ever since I was little, so I don't usually mind the fire alarm. That morning, however, I could have done without it, especially since Woofer went crazy and started barking at the alarm clock. I switched it off and turned to Woofer.

"Woofer. Be quiet!"

He lay down with a wounded expression. Oscar slept on unperturbed.

I sat up in bed and poked him with my big toe.

"Oscar," I said. "Rise and shine."

He just rolled over, still sound asleep. What did it take to rouse him? An anti-tank missile?

I got up slowly and made my way to the window. It had snowed while we'd been asleep – not masses, but a fine scattering of powder that made our otherwise rather dull courtyard look like a scene from a Christmas card. The washing lines wore a white ruff of hoar frost and the brown beech hedges looked like they'd been dusted with icing sugar. It was just starting to get light and the only tracks in the snow were from an animal, but I couldn't see whether it was a dog, cat or possibly even a fox.

Then I stopped mid-yawn. And stood very still. Very, very still indeed.

The animal tracks formed a pattern. Not a very accurate one. Not as if a person had written in the snow. Even so, I had no doubt that they were letters.

REM EMBERVIR IDI AN

"Oscar!"

I grabbed him and kept shaking him until he was at least so awake that he tried to push me away, while he grumbled sleepily: "Gerrofffme!" Or something like that, anyway.

"Get up, Oscar. Look!"

I practically dragged him to the window.

"Hey!" he exclaimed with delight. "It's been snowing!"

"Yes, but look at the tracks."

"Cool, aren't they? Do you think it was a fox?"

"Can't you see what it says?"

He squinted at the tracks and frowned.

"Says? It doesn't say anything. Clara, it was just an animal."

He couldn't see it. I didn't understand how come he couldn't, because to me it was glaringly obvious, even in the winter morning gloom, with just the glow from the street lamp to read it by.

REM EMBERVIR IDI AN

Remember Viridian.

"Gosh, I'm starving," Oscar said.

"But can't you see what it says?" I said again. "Remember Viridian!"

He just looked at me as if I'd lost my mind.

CHAPTER 7

Being Walked All Over

Mum said cycling in this weather was too risky, so she drove us to school in our little Kia. We made a stop outside Oscar's block in Jupiter Street, so he could take Woofer up to the flat, change his clothes, and pick up a book he needed.

"What did your mother say?" my mum asked when he got back in the car.

"Nothing," Oscar said. "She'd already gone to work. She says she gets much more done if she turns up before everybody else."

"Does she do that a lot?" I asked, thinking how much I would miss it if Mum and I didn't have our sleepy little ritual at the breakfast table. It wasn't that we said very much to each other, but I always got a quick morning hug and a noisy, tickly, raspberry on my neck while she pottered around making coffee, setting out muesli and toasting bread rolls in our mini oven.

"No, mostly when I'm at my dad's," Oscar said.

Mum wasn't the only one to take her car this morning, so it was crowded outside the school gates.

"There's nowhere for me to park," she said. "It'll have to be a stop-and-hop today. Are you ready?"

"Sure, sure," said Oscar, who was already scouting through the rear window for his friends.

Mum stopped and we hopped.

"Have a nice day," Mum called out, and drove on the moment we had shut the car door. The car behind her was already sounding its horn. I waved, but I don't think she saw me.

"Alex!" Oscar called out to one of his classmates. "Hey, Alex..." He ran ahead. I followed behind, plodding along at a more reluctant pace. Most of the snow in the school playground had already been trampled into a thin grey slush that spattered everything and everybody when you ran through it. Now what was my first lesson again? My brain felt like foam rubber.

Some of the boys from Year 10 were having a snowball fight. Or, more accurately, an ice-ball fight because the slush turned into grey, rocky lumps of ice when you pressed it hard enough. I stopped in my tracks. I had no wish to be caught in the crossfire.

Oscar had realized that I was lagging behind. He slapped Alex on the back of his shoulder with a wet, woollen mitten, making a loud splat.

"Be with you in a sec."

"You off to rescue your girlfriend, then?" Alex said, looking put out.

"She's not my girlfriend," Oscar said calmly. He was used to being teased about it. "Clara, get a move on."

I couldn't move. I just stood there staring at the older boys, one in particular. Martin. Martin from Year 10. Not because he was bigger than the other Year 10s, or much stronger for that matter. He was just meaner.

"Clara..."

By now Oscar had reached me. He turned to see what I was looking at. "Oh, drat," he muttered. Even Oscar was a little scared of Martin.

The bell went, but Martin and his fellow snowball fighters ignored the shrill ringing and kept up their strafing. They were no longer aiming at each other, but at anyone who tried to get through the door to B Block. Lumps of ice crisscrossed the air and we could hear cries of pain and howling when they found their targets.

"Clara, they're only snowballs," Oscar said. "You're a wildwitch. Surely you're not scared of being hit by a measly little snowball?"

But I was.

"Come on," he urged me. "We'll make a run for it. If we get hit, I'm sure we'll survive."

He slapped me on my shoulder, less hard and loud than when he slapped Alex. Then he set off at full tilt and somehow I too managed to peel my boots off the tarmac and follow him. I narrowed my eyes so that I could see only the ground in front of me and expected at any minute to be struck by a wet, hard ball of ice.

I wasn't. Something much worse happened.

Just as I was about to run up the steps and through the door, I slammed into something. Someone. I lost my footing and fell, arms flailing.

The pain wasn't the problem. My puffer jacket cushioned most of the impact, but I bashed my knee against a step and when I sat up, I saw that I had ripped my leggings. But that wasn't the worst part. The worst part was that the person I had run into was Martin.

Slowly he got to his feet. His skater trousers were wet from slush.

"What's up, Martin," the bravest of his friends called out. "Wet yourself, did you?"

Forced laughter erupted from the group, croaky and a little nervous. I just sat on the steps while he loomed over me; he looked huge as I stared up from below, and I couldn't make out his face very clearly, he was so close to me that a wide stretch of black polar jacket was almost the only thing I could see, that and two broad, bare hands, wet and fiery red from squeezing snowballs together.

"Loser," he snarled at me. "Look where you're going."

I usually do. I would always give a wide berth to anything that looked like trouble. I was rarely bullied or teased, mainly because I was so good at not standing out. Before you can tease someone, you first have to notice they are there.

Except now Martin had noticed me. And then some.

He bent over me and now I could see his face, almost as red as his hands; his eyes were strangely swollen and reduced to glittering cracks in all the red. He scooped up a handful of filthy slush from the steps. I barely had time to close my own eyes before the icy mixture of gravel, salt and melting snow was rubbed into my face. Then he stepped over me and walked off, seemingly indifferent to his entourage. They followed and made a big deal out of trampling me as if I wasn't there. One knee hit my side, a couple of them slapped me across the back of my head with wet mittens, and one boy stamped on my foot.

"Oi. Leave her alone!"

It was Oscar, of course, who earned himself a slap with a mitten in passing, but none of them stopped. The message was clear: I was someone you could walk all over, an insignificant little nobody who got what she deserved for failing to get out of the way quickly enough. Have a nice day, Mum had said. Yeah, right.

"They're the losers," Oscar said through clenched teeth as he helped me back on my feet. "Are you OK?"

"Yes," I muttered. Wet, filthy and with a face that felt as if it had been scoured with wet sandpaper. But apart from that OK.

"Why didn't you do something?" Oscar said. "Make them go away, just like the seagulls, or some other wildwitch trick. You just let them... walk all over you."

"It doesn't work like that," I said. "You make it sound as if I can just magic them away. I can't."

"Your Aunt Isa would never have let them walk all over *her*," he insisted.

Well, no. I would have liked to see them try...

"I'm not Aunt Isa."

"No, and you never will be if you don't stand up for yourself, Clara."

I was starting to regret ever telling Oscar about the wildwitches. I'd just had a totally rotten start to my day and now I'd be spending most of the morning in wet and filthy clothing. And Oscar was making it sound like it was all my own fault. That hurt. Much more than my foot and my knee and my snow-scoured face.

"What have I done?" I said. "Why are you being like that? You always…" I stopped myself just before I said "look out for me" because it would have sounded pathetic. But it was true. He'd always protected me. Ever since we were toddlers in the sandpit; he'd always defended me, and he put up with being teased by the others who would gleefully claim that we were snogging even though we had never done any such thing. Oscar was my friend, and he happened to be a boy. That didn't make him my boyfriend. Once, one warm afternoon during the summer holidays a long time ago when we were seven or eight years old, we had even sworn a blood oath, with Oscar making a small cut in his arm and in mine, with his grandfather's old pocket knife. I think Oscar had seen it in a movie somewhere.

Oscar heaved a sigh.

"I just don't get it," he said. "You can do all those really cool things. Shanaia says Chimera is afraid of you. But you still won't help her get Westmark back. And now you're letting that half-brain Martin and his moronic friends walk all over you. Clara, get a grip. It would be different if you couldn't defend yourself. But you can."

"You're right," I said. "You don't get it. If it's that easy, why don't *you* do it?"

I picked up my bag and brushed off the worst of the slush. I couldn't even look at him and my eyes were stinging. I didn't want to fall out with him. It was a horrible feeling that tore at my insides, as if I had just swallowed a whole box of thumb tacks. But he'd always known what I was like, and he used to like me just as I was. Why did he now suddenly want me to be someone else?

CHAPTER 8

It Gets Worse

I spent most of the day worrying about what Oscar had said. It still felt unfair. What on earth made him think I could take on Martin the Meanie? He was in Year 10. He was half a head taller than me. And he had a bunch of stupid friends, all of them bigger and stronger than me.

And if I couldn't stand up to Martin, how could anyone think I'd be able to take on Chimera? I felt sorry for Shanaia. I really did. Only there was nothing I could do about it.

Remember.

The thought crept into my mind halfway through Maths; it was nothing but a whisper. Nothing like Cat's usual loud and unmistakable messages. That's why I didn't notice him straight away.

Remember. Vi.

I rubbed my sore face with both hands. My head felt strange and heavy, and I kept wanting to go to sleep.

Ri.

What? I sat up with a jolt.

"Who let that cat in?"

Ruler-Rita, my scary Maths teacher, was pointing at my backpack on the floor. Or, more accurately, at the creature draping itself across it, like a furry cover.

"Cat!"

He got up, arched his back and dashed my leg with his broad paw.

Di.

And then he disappeared.

And I mean *disappeared*.

One moment he was there, a black, furry, solid, warm, feline body with gleaming yellow eyes; the next there was only a slowly dispersing cat-sized blob of fog, like a smoke signal disappearing in the sky.

Ruler-Rita stopped in her tracks, still with an accusatory finger pointing at my backpack. I had never seen a teacher quite that gobsmacked before.

"It... it..." she stuttered.

"Cat?" I said, only slightly less flustered. "Eh... what cat?"

She blinked a couple of times. Then she slowly lowered her pointing arm.

"Nothing..." she said feebly. "I... I just thought that..."

Although she wasn't my favourite teacher, I felt vaguely sorry for her. But I didn't say anything. I had finally worked out how Cat could come and go as he pleased, even in enclosed spaces. He used the wildways. He seemed to be able to open a passage into the wildways exactly where he wanted to, and to do it within only a second or two. Had he been a wildwitch rather than an animal, he would have been better than Aunt Isa. Or better at turning up and disappearing, at any rate. I couldn't help shuddering a little. Ever since I was three or four years old, I had wanted a pet – ideally a dog, but Mum had always said that our flat was too small. Then Cat had entered our lives, and she put up with him, though they weren't exactly bosom pals. So now I had Cat – or more accurately, he had me. And warm and fuzzy notions of him being *any* sort of pet would be very very foolish indeed.

Remember. Vi. Ri. Di.

REM EMBERVIR IDI AN

Remember Viridian.

Perhaps it wasn't an urban fox that had left those tracks in the snow. Perhaps it was Cat. But if he wanted me to "remember Viridian", why didn't he just say so? Why the mysterious tracks in the snow and this strange, strangled whisper as if he could barely get the syllables out? He'd never had any trouble getting my attention when he wanted it in the past.

"You can start the exercises on pages thirty-two and thirty-three now," Ruler-Rita said. "Anything you don't get done in class, you'll need to finish at home."

"But I don't understand the bit about the triangles," said Louise.

"Oh, do try a little harder, Louise. I've already explained it twice!"

Except that she hadn't. She'd stopped halfway through the second time because of Cat.

Why was Viridian so important? So important that Cat had appeared in the middle of a lesson, something he'd never done before. Neither Shanaia nor Aunt Isa had ever thought it worth mentioning. It seemed almost as if they'd forgotten all about it.

But Chimera had said it. Twice to me and once to Shanaia. So surely it had to mean something?

There was a general stir and shuffle as people found their pencil cases and opened their Maths books.

"Why is she being so weird? I was only asking..." Louise said in a stage whisper, loud enough for everyone to hear. Ruler-Rita was staring into the air and frowning as if sure she'd forgotten something important. She didn't say another word about Cat.

I waited for Oscar at our usual place by the bike shed, even though we hadn't cycled to school today. Tiny white snowflakes had started falling from the grey sky, and I got quite cold standing still. At length he appeared with Alex. I'd really hoped that he would be on his own. I'm not a big fan of Alex and I needed to talk to Oscar. The thumb tack sensation was still troubling me, and I desperately wanted things between us to be OK again.

But the first thing that happened was that Alex put on a broad grin and pointed a mitten at me.

"Oscar says you think you're some sort of witch."

He might as well have kicked me in the stomach. I felt all the air leaving my lungs in a huge, painful gasp, and I stared at Oscar in disbelief.

"No," he protested. "That's not what I said..."

He flapped his hands helplessly as if trying to erase the words. Alex ignored him.

"Do a trick," Alex said, still with that big grin plastered all over his face; it was clear he thought it was the best joke he had heard in ages. "Come on, Clara. Show us a little magic."

Three girls from Oscar's class had stopped on their way out of the school gates.

"I think her magic only works on Oscar," sniggered one of them, a tall, skinny, dark-haired girl called Caroline. And then they all three giggled and walked on, talking rather loudly to each other.

"My cousin used to think she could make herself invisible by closing her eyes," one of them said. "But then again she was only four years old at the time."

Oscar glanced after them desperately.

"I didn't mean to," he said. "It just sort of... I did tell him..." Then he suddenly turned to Alex and slammed his fist into his chest. "I told you not to *tell* anyone..."

"Ouch!" Alex shoved Oscar away. "Don't you go hitting *me*!"

I didn't see what happened next. I heard slaps and thumping muffled by puffer jackets and the scraping of boots on tarmac, so I think they got into a scuffle. But I didn't turn around or stop, not even when Oscar called out after me.

"Clara! Wait. Please let me explain..."

My legs felt as if they had been made from wood. Thumb tacks pierced and tore at my stomach and my throat. I had no wish whatsoever to hear him try to explain why he had told most of his class that Clara thought she was a witch.

CHAPTER 9

Bad Dreams

"Dad called," Mum said as I came through the door. "I think he was a bit upset that you just disappeared last night and never came back."

"Sorry," I mumbled.

"What did you say?"

"Sorry!" I said, louder this time. In fact, a little too loud. "Sorry, sorry, sorry, sorry..."

"Mousie! What's the matter with you?" She appeared in the doorway to her study. "There's no call for that."

But I couldn't handle disappointing any more people right now. Shanaia was upset. Mum was upset. Dad was upset. I'd fallen out with Oscar. And it seemed it was all my fault. Because they all wanted me to be someone else, someone bigger or smaller than I really was. Shanaia and Oscar wanted me to be bigger and more like Aunt Isa, and Mum and Dad would rather that I stopped acting weird and wildwitchy, and went back to being their little Mousie.

I could do neither.

I looked at Mum still standing in the doorway, expecting some sort of response.

"I'm not feeling too good," I said, which was the truth. "I think I have a fever..."

Oh no. That was clearly the wrong thing to say. I could practically see the fear grow in her eyes. It was less than six months ago that I had been seriously ill with Cat Scratch Disease, so ill that Mum had driven me to Aunt Isa's, despite having kept me away from her wildwitch big sister for all the twelve years of my life until then.

"Let me see." She placed her hand on my forehead for a moment. "You don't feel hot," she said, looking relieved. "Does it hurt anywhere?"

Only on the inside. But I didn't say that.

"I just don't feel too good," I said again. "I think I'll go to bed now."

It was only three o'clock in the afternoon, but all she did was nod.

"All right then, you didn't get much sleep last night," she said. "Perhaps that's all it is."

I crawled into my bed, fully clothed, and pulled the duvet right up to my ears. The grey winter light coming from the window was so faint that my things, my teddies and books, my computer, the Mickey Mouse alarm clock and the Anglepoise lamp on my desk were reduced to black outlines. I closed my eyes.

I don't know if I fell asleep properly, but I started dreaming straight away. At first I had a really weird dream where Mum, Dad, Shanaia and Oscar were making gingerbread men with different-sized biscuit cutters, while arguing over how big they should be. And then a more realistic, but far more terrifying dream.

I dreamt that Oscar had taken Woofer for a walk in Jupiter Park, across the road from Jupiter Street. His seagull-scratched face was so glum that he looked almost sad, or as sad as it's possible to look when you've been born with what my mum once called "the cheeriest face on the planet". Suddenly Woofer started barking like mad. Woof, woof, woof; loud, angry, go-away barking. Oscar looked about him, but could see nothing worth barking at. Dense snow had started falling, and he pulled up the hood of his sweatshirt and hushed Woofer. Then, without warning, Woofer fell silent. He stood rigid and very still for a moment. Then he set off with such determination that Oscar struggled to keep up. I watched Oscar say something to him, but the sound had suddenly disappeared, as if I were watching the telly on mute. Oscar tried to get Woofer to stop. He yanked the leash and dug in his heels, but Woofer simply carried on, and the leash slipped out of Oscar's hands.

"Woofer! Woofer!!" A tiny, tinny cry. The sound hadn't disappeared altogether, it was merely very weak.

Woofer accelerated to a doggy gallop. There was something odd and stiff about his movements, very different from his normal, happy labrador clumsiness. The snow whirled up around him and condensed into a pale grey hoary fog, and suddenly, mid-gallop, I lost sight of him.

Oscar stopped in his tracks. He stared at the whirl of snow and fog that had swallowed up his dog. He took a few steps and then he hesitated again.

Don't go in there, I tried calling out, but of course I wasn't there, I wasn't in the dream. I was just the one dreaming it.

Woof. Woof.

A barely audible barking was coming from inside the fog. Oscar started running and after only a few paces vanished into the glittering, snow-dotted wildways fog. There was nothing I could do to stop him.

"Woofer!" he called out. And then he was gone.

My room was almost completely dark when I woke up or came round or whatever it was I did. The luminous hands on the Mickey Mouse clock both pointed in the general direction of the number six, one hand slightly ahead of the other.

I could hear Mum talking on the phone. Perhaps that had woken me up.

"... no, she's here," she said. "She's been here ever since she came home from school. She's a little under the weather, I think." There was a pause while she listened to what the caller was saying. "I'll ask," she then said. "I'll ring you back."

Soon afterwards she knocked lightly on the door to my room and opened it.

"Mousie," she said. "Oscar's mum is asking if you know where Oscar is."

CHAPTER 10

Missing

"**I** work too much," said Oscar's mum in a flat, feeble tone which sounded nothing like her normal voice. "He spends too much time home alone. Why wasn't I with him? Do you have any idea where he could be?"

She was sitting in our kitchen, one hand permanently clutching her mobile. She was still wearing her work clothes: a smart dark jacket and a skirt, tights and high-heeled shoes. Her blonde hair was scraped away from her face and gathered at the back with a silver clip.

"He's probably just gone home with a friend, don't you think?" my mum suggested.

"But what about... the dog..."

Oscar had taken Woofer for a walk as he always did when he came home from school. He'd said hello to old Mrs Percival and her poodle at the entrance to Jupiter Park. No one had seen him since. And now I was left with a leaden feeling that my dream hadn't been a dream at all. I didn't think for one minute that Oscar was with a friend. I was convinced that he had followed Woofer into the fog of the wildways. I'd tried calling Aunt Isa six times now, but as usual to no avail.

"Mum..."

"Yes, Mouse?"

"Please may I go to the park to look for him?"

"No, sweetheart. Not now. It's too dark."

Oscar's mum emitted a small sound, a strangled, sniffling sob. "It's true. I work far too much," she said again, as if that would explain everything. My mum stroked her back and mumbled something comforting.

They'd called the police. I'd listened while Oscar's mum explained the situation and described what Oscar looked like. When she needed to tell them what he'd been wearing, she had to ask me because she hadn't been home when he got dressed that morning. Which was when she had started talking about working too much, as if she believed this was somehow all her fault.

The duty officer had dispatched a police officer who wrote a report and promised to circulate a missing persons notice, but I didn't think there was much the police could do.

I went to my room and put on some music. Not because I felt like listening to it, but because I needed some noise. A note, I thought. At the very least I should leave a note. "Gone to find Oscar," I wrote in big felt tip letters on a piece of squared paper from my Maths exercise book. "I think I know where he is. Don't worry. Clara xxx." I left the note on my bed, so Mum couldn't help seeing the message when she eventually realized that I was gone.

Now, it wasn't that I felt any braver than usual. But Oscar had never gone missing before. And I was convinced that the police could search until the cows came home without ever finding him. Not unless one of them happened to be a wildwitch...

I tiptoed out into the hallway, got my jacket and waterproofs from the peg and turned the latch as softly as possible. Then I opened and shut the door quietly, and tiptoed down the stairs one cautious step at a time. I'm fairly sure they didn't hear me leave.

I sat down on the bottom step, put on my puffer jacket and pulled my waterproofs on over my thin leggings. It was cold outside and the slush was starting to freeze. The pavement was covered by a slick, black skin of ice, and my breath turned to frosty puffs of mist in the air in front of me. I walked along the whole block and crossed Saturn Street, which ran along one side of Jupiter Park. There was no traffic and hardly any people around unless you counted the caretaker and his snow-blower.

I opened the gate to the park.

"Oscar?" I called out tentatively. But of course it was never going to be that easy.

The gravel path and the grass glittered with frost, and twigs and branches everywhere gleamed white in the glow of the street lamps. Blades of grass crunched and broke under my feet, so that I left a trail of dark footprints across the grass.

"Oscar!"

I knew perfectly well it wouldn't be that easy. This called for a completely different kind of search.

I stopped in the middle of the park, as far as possible from the roads and the houses that surrounded it. I closed my eyes. I waited until the distant hum of traffic and the more immediate roar of the snow-blower began to fade away.

"Cat..." I whispered. "You have to help me."

He turned up almost immediately. Suddenly I could feel his warm head against my leg and a silent question mark in my head. He wanted to know why I'd called him.

"I can't find my way through the wildways," I said quietly. "But you can..."

It took less than ten minutes. But they were ten terrifying, fearful, cold and confusing minutes. My eyes were stinging. I was so scared of losing sight of Cat that I didn't even dare blink.

He walked in front of me with his tail raised and his fur bristling. I followed him into the foggy land of the wildways. I tried calling out, but could manage only a pathetic whimper.

"Oscar..."

Cat turned his head and hissed. He wanted me to be quiet. We weren't the only ones travelling the wildways tonight.

At length trees and frosted grass began to appear in the fog. I heard an owl call and I wondered if it was Hoot-Hoot out hunting mice. And then we were there, in a shorter space of time than it took me to cycle to school every morning. The brook, the meadow, the woods and the farmhouse with a thin plume of smoke rising from the chimney... I drew a huge sigh of relief. I'd succeeded. I'd done it – or rather: Cat had done it. Strictly speaking, all I'd done was traipse along behind him.

Star whinnied sleepily from the stable, but I made a beeline across the farmyard to the house. I could see that the light was on in the living room; it seemed Aunt Isa hadn't gone to bed yet, though it was quite late.

The door of the house was ajar. Sometimes when you tried to close it, it refused to shut properly, it needed an extra tug and a small lift upwards. It had taken me a few days to learn the knack. I pushed it fully open.

"Aunt Isa..." I called out softly.

It was at this point that I realized something was wrong. Where was Bumble? Why hadn't he come bouncing, bursting with welcoming canine joy, trying to knock me over and so make it easier for him to lick my face? And why wasn't the door shut properly – after all, Aunt Isa certainly had the knack.

I entered the living room expecting the worst.

A solitary paraffin lamp was standing on the table beside the sofa, giving off a muted light. There was also a faint reddish glow from the embers in the wood burner. The patchwork quilt, which had covered Shanaia when she'd been resting on the sofa, was now lying in the middle of the floor and, when I stepped closer, I accidentally kicked a dropped and upended teacup. Cat hissed and puffed out his fur, making him almost twice his usual size.

Then I spotted the ferret. It lay very still, slumped up against the wall, with half-closed eyes and bared teeth. I didn't need to touch it to know that it was dead.

CHAPTER 11

The Empty House

I stared at Shanaia's dead ferret. Cat walked up to it and sniffed the motionless body before making a muted, indeterminable cat sound, a subdued mooooowwwwwrrrrrr. I had never heard Cat say anything as simple and cartoon-like as *meow*.

"What happened?" I whispered, but he made no reply.

The house was quiet. The fire in the log burner crackled faintly, but otherwise there was nothing, no voices, no footsteps, not even the creaking of the woodwork.

"Aunt Isa!" I called out so loud that I even frightened myself. But deep down I knew that no one would answer.

It's so unfair, said a tiny, resentful voice inside me. I finally do something dangerous and brave, walking all alone – apart from Cat, admittedly – along the wildways to Aunt Isa's house because Oscar was in danger, and I thought that Aunt Isa was the only one who could help me. And then she wasn't even here.

I knew I was being childish. Oscar was gone. Something terrible had happened in the farmhouse, Aunt Isa was gone, Shanaia was gone, and her poor little ferret was dead... All of which was obviously far more important than how I was feeling right now. But I'd pretty much convinced myself that all I had to do was get to Aunt Isa's – and that had been hard enough – then she would fix the rest.

Oh, no. What if she hadn't gone missing at all? What if she was lying somewhere, just as dead as the ferret...

I hadn't thought my heart could feel sicker or more terrified. But it could.

I turned up the wick of the paraffin lamp and carried it with me while I wandered from room to room – the kitchen, the small bathroom with the hissing water heater, the creaking stairs leading to the attic and my own little room with the round window. There was no one, no dead or unconscious Aunt Isa – fortunately – nor any mysterious monsters or wicked foes lying in wait to ambush me. The house was deserted.

What on earth should I do? Wait? Start searching? I had no idea where to even begin. And it was pitch black outside.

I found a tea towel in the kitchen and used it to

carefully wrap up the small, stiff body of the ferret. Then I put it in one of the cardboard boxes Aunt Isa kept for injured or sick little creatures and put the box in the boot room. If Shanaia came back, I thought, then she might want to bury it. I felt I ought to write something on the box. Name, date of birth, something along those lines – like an inscription on a gravestone, I guess. But I couldn't remember the name of the ferret. I didn't even know whether it was a he or she. It's not so easy to tell with ferrets.

I opened the door of the log burner and chucked more wood on the fire, picked up the overturned teacup and the patchwork quilt, leaving it neatly folded on one end of the sofa. It seemed to calm me down, doing everyday things – putting logs on the fire, tidying up. I decided that making a cup of tea might settle me even more.

I tried. But I ended up sitting in an armchair staring at the cup while the tea slowly stopped steaming and grew cold.

"Cat?" I whispered and stroked his coarse, black back. "What am I going to do?"

His fur bristled even more, and he stiffened and tensed on my lap. I could feel his claws against my thigh.

Re. Member. He hissed from the exhaustion. *Remember.*

"Viridian?"

The tension eased and he rolled onto his back, so I could scratch his tummy. *Yes. Remember.*

"But I don't know what that means."

He swatted me with his paw – no claws, but quite firmly, as when a mother cat disciplines a kitten. I concluded he thought I was being very dim-witted. Then his paw suddenly shot out and he sank one claw into my thumb – only a tiny scratch, but enough for a single, ruby-red drop to balloon on my skin.

"Cat!" I tried pushing him away, but he refused to budge. I raised my hand to my mouth and sucked up the drop of blood. The moment the salty, iron taste spread across my tongue, Cat's voice echoed in my head again: *Remember.*

"Blood," I said spontaneously. "The blood of Viridian."

He purred. *At last.*

"But why?" I insisted. "I still don't know what it means. Why can't you just tell me?"

I got the distinct impression that had he been human, he would have clutched his head and kicked something very heavy.

I sat like that, waiting, for hours. Right until the windows changed from black to grey because it was dawning outside. But Aunt Isa and Shanaia didn't come back, and all the thoughts I was having meanwhile made me none the wiser.

When it had grown so light that I was able to go outside without tripping over every single fallen branch, I climbed to the top of the hill behind the stable to call my mum, who would undoubtedly be worried sick despite the note I'd left for her.

As soon as the display showed even a few bars of coverage, two text messages pinged to announce their arrival. One was from my mum, naturally. *Where are you?* It said. *Call me!*

The second was from Aunt Isa.

WESTMARK, it said in capital letters. That was all, nothing like Come or Help or Watch out for Chimera! Just the one word. It was up to me to decide what to do about it.

I thought about the picture Shanaia had shown me. The long coastline and the cliffs, the silky sea. The house at the edge of the world, the seagulls hovering in the wind. A strange sense of certainty grew inside me. That was where they were now. Oscar, Shanaia and Aunt Isa. And Bumble. If I wanted to find them, that was where I would have to go.

But... Chimera would also be there.

CHAPTER 12

Wild Dogs

The first sound to break the chilly silence of the wildways was that of the sea. Quietly lapping waves and the cry of a solitary seagull, one long and four short: *uuuuuuuuuuurrr – urr urr urr urr*. Then I heard crunching under my feet as crisp crusts of ice cracked when I stepped on them. Dark cliffs loomed to my right and at their foot a frosty, yellow forest of tall reeds poked up through the ice. To my left the waves whispered quietly across the shore under a thin, oily membrane of ice.

I'd arrived. I recognized the place from Shanaia's picture and, although I couldn't see the house, it must be hiding somewhere in front of me, a little further along the shore.

Cat had led me through the wildways fog, never more than a few paces ahead of me. I couldn't see him right now, and yet I sensed that he was nearby.

I was here. I was really here. I was walking along Westmark's shoreline, despite thinking I would never dare. I still didn't dare, not really. I was just doing it anyway. And I didn't believe for one moment that I could take on Chimera. I felt no bigger or stronger or braver than before. But the thought of going back to Mercury Street and pretending nothing had happened while the police and Oscar's mum kept searching and never found him because they were looking in the wrong place... it was unthinkable. Much worse than being here, all alone, except for Cat perhaps, and waiting for Chimera to notice me.

I didn't have any kind of clever plan. I could, of course, try to sneak as close as possible to the house without being seen, but if the soul-stripped animals had caught Shanaia in under an hour, it would surely take even less than that before they dug their claws into me. After all, Shanaia was born and bred here, and besides – although she was young – she was a fully trained wildwitch. My one slender hope was that Shanaia had been right when she'd said that for some reason the soul-stripped animals wouldn't touch me.

The frozen shore suddenly looked exposed and bare. The sky and the sea, the ice and the sand, and not a bush or tree for miles around. The only hiding place was inside the jungle of whispering, yellow reeds, but I couldn't go there, the ice crust wasn't strong enough to support my weight, nor would I be able to tell if I was still walking in the right direction.

So I stayed on the shore, but kept close to the reed forest. I didn't know if it made a difference. The seagulls would probably detect me no matter what I did. And what was it Shanaia had said about wild dogs?

I'd barely finished the thought when I heard a loud, yipping bark. It was coming from behind me, somewhere on the other side of the reeds, I thought. I'd stopped instinctively at the sound, but what could I do apart from walk on? Run? The dogs could probably run at more than twice my speed. *Go away*, I whispered in my mind. *Go away, go away, go away*.

The reeds rustled. And, although I'd decided not to, I suddenly found myself running. My wellies were heavy and clumsy, and the ice made it worse, either cracking under my weight, or, if it held, so slippery that I was constantly skidding and stumbling.

Yip-yip, yip-yip. More sharp barking – and gaining on me all the time. They were no longer only behind me, but also coming up on my right, through the reeds. "They surrounded me, and I couldn't escape." That was what Shanaia had said, and now the same was happening to me. I made a sharp left out onto the sandy shore where running would at least be easier. They might be able to see me better – but then I would also be able to see them.

The frosty air stung my lungs. Now I might not be the worst in our class at PE, but I'm far from the best either, and the school's annual fitness run is always something of an ordeal. If I get out of this alive, I vowed, I'm going to take up running and healthy eating. Cross my heart! My boots flopped around my calves, and my thighs felt heavy, cold and stiff.

Yip-yip, yip-yip!

This time, the barking was coming from the reeds just in front of me. Four or five fox-like creatures emerged from the reeds and ran out onto the shore.

I stopped. The air was wheezing in and out of my chest and I was sweating so hard that the T-shirt under my jumper and puffer jacket was sticking to my armpits and my back as if glued there. But they're not very big, I thought. Smaller than foxes, in fact. Tawny with dark spots on their flanks, black-rimmed, pointy, triangular ears and a dark mask around their eyes. Almost cute. For a moment I felt daft for being so scared and trying to outrun them. That was before I noticed the red glow in their eyes. They weren't blood red, like the seagulls' eyes had been, but it was there, a fiery, red glint in the dark.

The first five wild dogs were only the vanguard. Behind me, and from the forest of reeds to my right, at least twenty more dogs poured out onto the shore, their heads lowered and their legs strangely stiff. They approached slowly, one step at a time. There was no longer any reason for them to hurry, I wasn't going anywhere. They surrounded me just as easily as they'd surrounded Shanaia.

"Cat," I whispered. "Cat, are you there? Help me now!"

Remember.

That was all. That was all the help I got.

The dogs moved closer, also to each other, until they formed a full circle. A circle with me in the middle. Then I heard a final, sharp: "Yip!" from one of them, an older bitch with a grizzled face and a lop-sided, torn ear, and they pounced as one.

Lop-Ear struck me just below my chest like a furry cannonball. Other teeth closed around a calf, an arm, a welly. I shouted and lashed out at them, trying to stay on my feet, but they were tugging and pulling at my waterproofs, sleeves, boots, I was tugged and shoved and harried, and eventually dragged to my knees, and then, seconds later, three or four dogs were on my back, and I collapsed under a pile of salivating jaws, tawny bodies and broad paws with strong, yellowish claws.

"**GO AWAY!**" My mouth was full of sand, I could hardly breathe. Spitting and coughing and writhing, I screamed "**GO AWAY**" as loud as I could, inside and out. But they weren't going anywhere.

They're going to maul me to death, I thought and panicked. Soon all that will be left of me will be a few stripped bones and a bloodstained patch of frozen sand.

Then I realized two things.

They were silent – there was no growling or snarling. And so far, none of them had bitten anything other than my clothes. They weren't trying to eat me. They just wanted me to lie still so they could restrain me. I ended up half on my back, half on my side, with Lop-Ear on top of me. She squatted and peed on my leg. Then her head shot forwards in a sudden and terrifying movement, and her jaws closed around my neck and chin, just hard enough for me to feel how sharp her fangs were.

I stopped shouting. Instead, I lay very still while hot dog pee seeped through my not-quite-water-proofs and the thinner leggings underneath, and I felt my leg grow wet. I closed my eyes. She kept her grip on my chin and throat for what seemed like an eternity, but perhaps it was seconds or minutes, I don't know.

Cat, I thought. You're supposed to protect me, aren't you? How can you let them do this?

And the worst part wasn't even that I was lying on the icy sand with dog pee on my leg and a set of jaws clamped around my throat. That was just the beginning. Because I was starting to realize why they didn't bite me properly, why they were only restraining me. Shanaia had said it: "They surrounded me, and I couldn't escape." They hadn't killed Shanaia either, they had only pinned her down while they waited, just as they were doing now.

While they waited for Chimera to arrive.

CHAPTER 13

Lop-Ear

How long? How long would it be before Chimera came? I'd seen her fly once, though other wild-witches claimed that not even wings as big as hers would be able to support the weight of a human – or something that had been human once. I stared at the leaden sky, but could see no wings other than those of the seagulls.

"Cat," I whispered. "Cat, help me."

I'd been crying and hadn't even noticed. Now I could feel the sand sticking to my cheeks, wet from tears and wild dog drool. But I couldn't see or hear Cat. Perhaps twenty-five wild dogs were too many to take on, even for him. Perhaps that explained why he'd stayed away.

They were eerily still, the dogs. Lop-Ear might have released her grip on my throat for the time being, but she was still lying across me with all her weight on my chest. Nine or ten dogs had their jaws clamped on my sleeves and waterproofs, so moving would mean dislodging forty or fifty kilos worth of dog. There was no way I could do that, not with my legs, and definitely not with my arms. None of them made a sound. They just held me down. Those that hadn't managed to get their teeth into something stood completely still while they waited. Not a single one of them shook itself or scratched an ear or sniffed or did the things that normal dogs do. "A heinous crime," Aunt Isa had called it, and it wasn't until now that I truly understood what she meant. It wasn't the same as controlling an animal, like when a person trains a dog or a horse. What Chimera had done to the dogs was something completely different. She'd taken them over. She'd stripped them of all their natural instincts, their canine nature, and turned them into small, remote-controlled robots. Aunt Isa was right. It really was heinous.

I heard Chimera before I saw her. A rush as if a thousand birds were taking off at once. But this wasn't a thousand birds, it was just one. A giant non-bird with a wingspan that shut out the sun.

Chimera.

I started resisting again. I couldn't help it, even though I didn't think it would be any use. And of course it only made Lop-Ear close her teeth around my throat again.

"Cat! *Cat!*"

Remember.

It was the only response he'd given me, the only help, and I had no idea what to do with it. I made a last, desperate attempt; I twisted my entire body violently, so violently, in fact, that Lop-Ear's teeth slipped and pierced my skin.

She tasted my blood.

I could feel it in a strange, internal way, as if my blood were still a part of me though it had left my body and was really nothing but a few drops of red liquid.

Now I'm not saying that I suddenly understood everything. Far from it. But something inside me stirred, an instinct, a dream, a... a hunch telling me that I knew something I'd merely forgotten.

"Viridian," I said. "Blood of Viridian."

Lop-Ear released me immediately. I saw it in her eyes; I *felt* it, almost as if she'd become a part of me. The blood-red glow in her eyes vanished. She became a dog once more. She was free.

She exploded into the faces of the other dogs, a snarling, barking, growling dog bomb. At once the eerie silence was blown to bits, the pack was no longer a collection of robots, but a huge, undulating dogfight with me in the centre. There was biting and merciless ripping, blood and fur flying everywhere, claws tearing, teeth rending. I curled up and tried to crawl out from under, protecting my face and my head as best I could.

Then suddenly the fight was over. Yipping loudly, most of the pack disappeared into the reeds, and only those most badly injured stayed behind. There were three of them. One was trying to follow the pack as best it could on three legs – its left front leg appeared to be broken. The second had had its throat ripped open and was practically dead already, only a few spasms causing its flank and rear legs to twitch.

The last dog was Lop-Ear. She lay on her side gasping, her jaws half-open. She had so many cuts and injuries that it was impossible to say which was the worst. Practically all of her spotted, tawny fur was stained with blood.

If I'd been able to save her, I would have done it.

A few minutes ago she'd held my neck in a mortal grip, like someone holding a knife to my throat. But she hadn't wanted to do it. And, in some strange way, she and I had connected the moment she tasted my blood, and she'd reacted instantly. She'd attacked the soul-stripped animals in the pack with all her strength, she'd fought until she could fight no more, and she'd been victorious. She'd set her pack free.

Her eyes were dimming. I could see she was dying, I could feel it. But I also knew that she was grateful. She would rather die a dog than live a soul-stripped monster. And her pack was free.

I put my hand on her neck, but I knew that it was no use. I couldn't stem the bleeding from all those bites. Her flanks trembled, and she grew still. She was gone.

I knelt by her side for a few seconds. Then I looked up, up at the sky, and clumsily rose to my feet so that at least I would be standing when Chimera arrived.

Except that she didn't come.

I spun around, frantically scanning the sky, but it was empty. There wasn't as much as a single seagull, and no sign of a giant human bird.

Chimera had turned back.

Fury washed through me like a burst of wildfire. Fury at what she had done to me, but even more at what she had done to Lop-Ear and her pack. For a brief moment I forgot that I was smaller and weaker than her, and that I was scared of her.

"Come on, then!" I yelled at the sky. "Come back here, and let's get it over with!"

No reply. No one came.

My pounding heart was starting to pound a lot less. My breathing relaxed. I started to get cold and still nothing happened. She wasn't coming.

At length I scraped a pit in the frozen sand so that I could bury Lop-Ear and her dead pack-brother. Lop-Ear probably couldn't care less about such silly rituals, but I was a human being, not a wild dog. I couldn't just abandon her to the seagulls and the crows even though that would have been the way of the wild. After all, she'd saved my life.

As I was digging, Cat came strolling along the shore as if nothing had happened. I stopped digging and glared at him.

"Why didn't you help me?" I demanded to know.

But I did.

He arched his back and yawned. There was something incredibly smug about him which made me even more furious.

"Go away," I said. "If that's your 'help', I'll manage without you."

He sat down on the sand and languidly started licking one paw. The message was loud and clear. He wasn't some lapdog that came running whenever I called, and he wasn't going away just because I told him to.

CHAPTER 14

Westmark

The house was bigger than it had looked in the picture. Four storeys high, with gables and dormers sticking out in all directions, six chimneys, and a weathervane in the shape of a predatory bird of some kind – a hawk or a falcon or possibly a buzzard. From a distance the house had looked black, but now that I was actually here, I could see that it had been painted a very dark, bog-water sort of green. Or, at least the top had, the part which was made from wood. The lower half had been built with dark grey stone. The same kind of stone had been used to construct the long wall that surrounded the garden, or whatever you would call the windblown cluster of pine trees, sloe bushes and brambles, heather and dog grass that seemed little different from the plant life growing outside the garden wall.

The path I was following led to a cemetery-style gate of rusty wrought iron. Bramble wound in and out of the bars and it was clear that the gate hadn't been opened for a long time. There had to be another entrance that was used more frequently, I thought. Or maybe not? After all, Chimera could simply fly in and out if she wanted to.

I stopped some distance from the gate, under cover of some pine trees that offered protection against the wind and hostile stares – that is, if anyone was watching. The sky was still as blank as a piece of paper – no seagulls, neither soul-stripped blood gulls nor the regular kind. Nor was there any sign of Chimera.

I couldn't understand it. I'd heard her, seen her. Why had she turned back? It would have been easier for her, of course, if the wild dogs had done the job for her and pinned me down until she came, but even without them I hardly represented a major challenge. When she'd captured me last autumn, it had taken her approximately fifteen seconds to floor me and put an iron collar around my neck. That I'd later escaped from her was more down to luck than skill.

But she'd turned back. And she hadn't reappeared. If the thought of it hadn't been so absurd, I'd have been tempted to think that Shanaia had been right when she said that Chimera was afraid of me. It made me feel a tiny bit tougher. As if I actually stood a chance...

The wind whistled in the grass and bent the branches of the pine trees so that their resinous smell filled my nostrils. I couldn't stand here forever, I told myself. I had only two options – go back or carry on.

The hinges on the gate squeaked when I pushed it open, or partly open – the bramble made it impossible to open it fully, but the gap was wide enough for me to slip through. The wall loomed on either side of me, tall and thick, so it was like walking into a medieval fortress.

Who builds a garden wall two metres tall and almost three metres wide, I wondered. I reached out my hand to touch the dark, crumbling stone. And that's when I realized that it wasn't a garden wall, but the remains of another building, bigger and more ancient than the old house awaiting me further ahead. Westmark was built on, and from, the ruins of something else, something which had been here long before the pine trees had grown, so long that the stones had been worn and weathered by centuries of wind, rain, salt spray and cold.

Kiiiiiiiiiiiiiirrr. A protracted, shrill cry made me look up. But it wasn't Chimera plunging towards me, her wings held stiffly up against the wind. It was the weathervane. My heart jumped up in my throat and, for a brief moment, it seemed as if the iron figure had truly come alive. Then I realized that it was more likely to have been a real bird all along, one that I'd mistaken for a weathervane because it had sat so still up on the swivel, a black silhouette against the snow-laden grey sky.

It was the kestrel. I was absolutely sure that it was the same bird, even though I probably wouldn't have been able to tell it apart from other kestrels if there had been more than one. Kiiiiiiiiiiiirrr. It swooped low over my head, but didn't land, neither on the wrist which I instinctively held up, nor on the branches of the pine trees. I didn't know what it wanted. But it wasn't an attack, and it had been close enough for me to see that it didn't have the blood-red glow of the soul-stripped in its yellow eyes.

"Was that supposed to be a welcome?" I muttered. "Or is that your way of telling me to get lost?"

It made no reply. It merely flew in a sweeping, wide arc across the grass, and turned into the wind to help with its ascent. For a moment it hung almost stationary in the up-draught over my head, then it flapped its barred wings a couple of times and returned to its spot on the weathervane.

Gooseberry bushes and small, crippled apple trees grew on either side of the path. It had to be the remnants of an orchard and a vegetable patch but it had been a long time since anyone had done the work necessary for it to remain a veg patch, but then again, it took a considerable stretch of the imagination to visualize Chimera on her knees, grubbing in the soil, planting cabbages and parsley. Was she even *able* to kneel? What would happen to her wings if she tried?

I peered up again, but there was still no sign of a giant bird woman. It should have reassured me, but it didn't. It just felt as if she was lying in wait somewhere I *couldn't* see her, and that was far worse.

There was a door at the gable of the house – or rather, in one of many gables and porches and bays which protruded from the main building. It was locked, but on a nail in the door frame hung a big, old-fashioned iron key that turned out to fit the lock. So what was the point of locking the door in the first place? Unless, of course, you didn't lock the door to keep thieves and other trespassers out, but to imprison someone or something within. Again, not a very comforting thought.

I entered a dim passage. On a row of pegs along one wall were jackets and raincoats, a straw hat and an old-fashioned yellow sou'wester – the type of rain hat worn by fishermen in very old pictures. Below were wooden clogs and wellington boots in different sizes and a wooden basket that was lined with newspaper and held some wizened onions. All very normal and everyday if it hadn't been for the cobwebs and the thick brown layer of dust and mould in the folds of the coats, the clogs and on top of the wellington boots. There was a glass-panelled overhead light that looked a bit like a ship's lantern, and a porcelain switch by the door frame – not likely to be approved by any modern safety board. I flicked it, but nothing happened. I wasn't really surprised.

I carried on up a small flight of stairs – just four steps – and through the next door. I had a strange urge to call out "hello?" or "hi!" or words to that effect, but I didn't. It would have been wonderful if Oscar or Aunt Isa had responded, but I feared it was more likely that I'd be heard by other, more hostile ears.

I found myself in a kitchen, a big old-fashioned one with an ancient cast-iron wood-burning cooker as well as an enormous gas stove. Dusty bunches of mummified herbs and braided onions hung from the ceiling beams, and big, heavy, enamelled iron pots and skillets dangled from hooks on the wall. In the corner was a pastel-yellow 1950s fridge which might not be so strange, apart from the fact that this one looked as if it really *was* from the 1950s, and not a fancy retro imitation.

"Go away."

The voice was weary, squeaky, and hoarse at the same time, and I leaped a foot. I had thought the room was deserted. I looked around frantically, but I still couldn't see anyone.

"Hello?" I ventured.

"Go away."

My heart was pounding against my ribcage. There was no one here, and yet I could hear the tired words, very clear and very close.

"Where are you?" I whispered. "I can't see you."

"Go away."

Then I spotted the birdcage hanging from a hook between the pots and pans. A parrot?

But it hadn't sounded like a parrot.

I retraced my steps to get a better look at what was inside the cage.

It was a bird. A big, glum bird-figure about the shape of an owl with untidy, grey-brown feathers. And yet at the same time, it wasn't. The face wasn't that of an owl. There was no beak, no dark owl eyes surrounded by pale feathers. Instead there was skin, eyebrows, human eyes, a human nose and mouth.

In a fit of morbid curiosity I had looked up "chimera" on the Internet during the Christmas holidays and found a lot of articles about chimeras – an ancient Greek word meaning crossing two animals into one creature. Or even more terrifying, an animal and a human being. Like this one.

"Go away," she said, sounding glum and sad, the tears flowing down her little girl's face in a steady, constant stream that left wet trails on her chest feathers.

My skin crawled. Birds are supposed to have beaks and talons. Not human faces and soft fingers where the talons are supposed to be.

"Who are you?" I asked.

"The Nothing."

"What?"

"The Nothing," she repeated.

"Don't you have a name?"

"Yes. That's what she calls me. The Nothing."

"She?" I said. "Do you mean Chimera?"

She nodded, a small, jerky movement, very birdlike.

"My mum," she then said.

CHAPTER 15

The Nothing

The chimera sat on her perch in the cage, looking dolefully at me as the tears continued to flow in a quiet trickle down her tiny, human face and onto the damp chest feathers.

"Chimera is your mum?" I asked her again to be absolutely sure.

"She made me," she said, with more of that small, jerky, bird nodding.

I stared at the human-bird creature. Her eyes were darker than Chimera's, golden-brown rather than predatory yellow, but her nose was just as curved and sharp. I could make out some family resemblance.

"But... why has she put you in a cage, then?"

"Because I was a failure. No part of me turned out to be really useful. I'm just... The Nothing." She flung out a wing. "Eventually she got fed up with me following her about all the time. I tried not to, but... I couldn't. It's really hard not to follow your mum, you know."

It was probably the saddest thing I'd ever heard. The worst part was almost that she spoke with such acceptance, as if Chimera's actions were entirely natural and justifiable.

Without warning she sneezed; the small, shrill sneeze of a kitten or a tiny dog. At the same time a thin, pale yellow stream shot out from under her tail feathers.

"I'b so bery, bery sorry," she said, then sniffled loudly to clear her nose. "I'm allergic to dust mites, and I... I can't really groom my own feathers."

The bottom of the cage was covered by a thick layer of bird poo and fallen feathers, I could see that now. And it made me very, very angry.

"You shouldn't have to put up with this," I seethed. "No one should live like this. No one should be called... that name." I searched for a door in the cage, but couldn't find any. I wondered if the cage had been constructed with The Nothing inside it. "Is there any way of opening this thing?"

"I don't think so," The Nothing said. "I don't think it's meant to be opened."

"We'll see about that," I said grimly. The bars were metal and fairly thick. I didn't think that I could bend them. However, the bottom of the cage seemed to be made from plywood. Perhaps I could saw or carve a hole in it? I looked around for a tool I could use, and my glance fell on a block next to the sink holding five or six cook's knives.

"Hold on," I said. I dragged a stool closer, climbed it and unhooked the birdcage.

"Help!" The Nothing screamed, bobbing wildly up and down on her perch. "I'll fall off, I'll fall off…"

"This… will only… take a minute," I panted. The cage was heavier than I had expected, but I managed to lug it to the kitchen table.

"I'm going to have to put it down on its side," I warned her.

"No! No!"

I ignored her cries of alarm and tipped the cage onto one side. A cloud of filth and feathers and bird droppings erupted, and The Nothing sneezed and pooed and flapped her wings, and her screams were now so piercing that I was tempted to stuff my ears with cotton wool. That is, if I'd had any.

"Now be quiet!" I ordered her, and then repeated, more calmly, this time: "It'll only take a minute, then you'll be free."

"Free?" The Nothing said in a strange, fumbling tone of voice. "What's that?"

"Wait and see." I grabbed one of the biggest knives and started hacking away at the base of the cage. With every hack The Nothing would leap awkwardly and then let out a small, frightened scream. The tip of the knife barely seemed to dent the wood, but after I had stabbed it six or seven times, one side suddenly came away from the metal hoop it was set into. I turned over the knife and bashed the handle as hard as I could against the wood, and with a crunch, the base separated from the frame of the cage and tilted like a cat flap. I grabbed the cage with one hand and the base with the other and pulled the whole thing apart, trying to ignore the sticky sensation of bird droppings, fresh and ancient, oozing through my fingers.

"There you go," I said. "You're free."

I hurled the bottom of the birdcage as far away as I could, and just managed to stop myself from wiping my fingers on my waterproofs.

The Nothing was balancing awkwardly on the bars of the upended cage and staring through the round hole where the bottom had been.

"Why did you do that?" she asked.

"What do you mean?"

"Why did you ruin my cage?"

"To set you free, of course!"

"Free?"

"Yes."

"But I don't know what that means. Please will you tell me what it means?"

I took a deep breath.

"Eh... it's... I guess it means that you make your own decisions. That you're able to do what you want."

"And I can do that now?"

"Yes. You're free."

She nodded twice.

"Very well. Then please would you open the door for me?" She nodded towards the exit.

"Why?"

"So I can go looking for my mum."

"No! I mean, I don't think that's a very good idea."

"Why not?"

"Because..." Because then she'll know where I am, I thought, but I had a strange feeling that Chimera already knew. "Because then she'll lock you up inside the cage again."

"I know."

"But... is that what you want?"

"No. But I want to be with my mum."

I shook my head slowly. "Why??"

"I don't know. That's just the way it is. I can't help following her."

"But you have to. You have to learn not to!"

"Why? Please open the door. I can't do it on my own."

"No! No, that's just not right. I won't let you!"

"But you just said..." The Nothing's voice wobbled. "You just said I could do what I wanted. Being free and all that. Wasn't that what it meant?"

"Yes. Or rather... You are free to do what you want, but there are still some things you shouldn't do, even if you feel like doing them. Do you understand?"

"Mmmhh... Like eating something that makes you sick?"

"Right. And although it might be really, really hard – you have to stop following Chimera. You have to find out where *you* want to go."

The Nothing sneezed. A couple of down feathers loosened from her plumage and fluttered onto the kitchen table.

"But I don't want to go anywhere," she said. "Except where my mum is."

I stared at the unkempt little chimera and felt a jab of irritation mix with my pity.

"Well, then you do that," I said at length. "If that really is all you want. But you'll have to open the door yourself."

I turned on one of the taps. The pipes hissed and gurgled, but eventually a stream of rusty water shot out of the tap. I washed my filthy hands. Then I stripped off my waterproofs and rinsed the trouser leg Lop-Ear had peed on. The Nothing sat very still all the while, watching everything I did with intense interest.

"You're so clever," she said admiringly. "You can clean your own plumage."

I didn't know how to respond to that, so I didn't. I hung my waterproofs across the back of a kitchen chair so they could dry. It was cold in here, but not as cold as outside, and besides, putting on wet trousers would only make the cold worse.

"Do you know if there are any peop... eh... anyone else in the house?" I asked.

"I think so," she said. "I've heard voices."

"For how long?"

"Since yesterday at least."

That could be Aunt Isa, I thought. And possibly Oscar as well. And Shanaia.

I dried my hands on a dusty tea towel, and cautiously opened the door at the other end of the kitchen, which proved to open onto a long, dark passage with rows of pegs along one wall and several abandoned, dusty coats. The Nothing followed me as best she could. She wasn't all that good at flying or walking on her fingerfeet; it turned into a clumsy, flapping gait. She sneezed. And pooed on the floor. And sneezed again. Feathers and dust flew everywhere.

"What are you doing?" I asked.

She flapped her wings to keep her balance, caught a wingtip on one of the coats and tripped, straightened up again, and stared at me with lost, golden-brown eyes.

"It's so hard not to follow someone," she said. "Please may I follow you instead?"

I guessed it was better than her following Chimera. And although I didn't really fancy having her small, flapping, sneezing, pooing figure at my heels, it was also impossible to say no.

"OK," I said. "But just to begin with. Until you learn. But you must begin to decide what you want to do. Do you understand?"

"Yes, yes," she said eagerly. "I promise."

I turned around to continue, when a thought came into my mind.

"Hey, eh..." I couldn't bring myself to call her The Nothing, not out loud. "Little friend."

"Friend?" she said. "What's that?"

"A friend is... someone you like." Seriously! Claiming I actually *liked* The Nothing was probably going too far. What was I getting myself into here?

"Like?" she said. "You mean... food you think tastes nice?"

"Eh, yes. Maybe. Or... not really... it's someone you're happy to see."

"Happy," she said. "I know what that is. I just haven't tried it all that much."

Pity welled into a painful lump in my throat. I swallowed and quickly returned to the question that I really wanted to ask.

"You said 'go away' when you spotted me. Several times. Why did you do that?"

"It wasn't something I made up," The Nothing said, looking terrified. "I said it only because the others did."

"What others?"

"Them. The house. They're in the house. They want you to go away." She looked at me with big, shiny eyes. "Can't you hear them?"

CHAPTER 16

The Sisters

"'Go away'," I said to The Nothing. "Are you sure that's what they said?"

"No," she began to waver. "Not if you don't think so."

But she was sure, or at least she had been before I started questioning her.

"Who are they?"

"I don't know," she said. "I've never seen them. I can only hear them... very faintly." She pointed a wingtip at her head. "In here."

I got goose pimples all the way down my spine. Now a lot of people might have dismissed it and concluded that The Nothing had lost her marbles in captivity, but I remembered the kestrel dive-bombing in front of me like a fighter plane. And since meeting Cat, I'd learned that not all the voices in your head are your own.

"What do they say?"

"Just 'go away'."

"Are they angry?"

"No. Not with you."

"Then why do they want me to leave?"

"I don't know."

I took a deep breath. Closed my eyes. Tried listening with my wildsense, and listen properly. But although I tried for several minutes, I picked up nothing but silence, which in an old house isn't really silence but a creaking, a whisper, a gurgling in the pipes.

Hang on. Wait.

Someone *was* here. Right on the other side of the door I was thinking of opening, there was life. But it was a strange form of life. I sensed many different breaths, many different hearts, and yet... oddly unified. Something was waiting, without stirring, and although I was convinced there was more than one life behind that door, they were all completely identical.

"Someone's in there," I said, pointing at the door. "Is that what you mean?"

"Oh no," The Nothing said. "That's just the sisters."

"Sisters?"

She nodded. "My sisters. They turned out better than me."

"And they're the ones who want me to leave?"

"Oh no," she said again. "They're not like that. It's... the others."

I closed my eyes. Tried to get past the still, waiting presence which The Nothing called her "sisters". It was difficult, it was as if they formed a wall around me, but faintly, ever so faintly, I began to sense...

Oscar.

There are times I get the feeling that he and I are connected by an incredibly thin, red thread, finer than a fishing line. Most of the time I can't see or feel it, but now that I concentrated... I was almost certain that it was him. *Almost*.

I opened the door – first only a crack, then when nothing happened, a little more.

On the other side of the door there was a hall with a large staircase leading all the way up to the top of the house. There wasn't very much light, only a single big round stained glass window above what I assumed must be the front door. Several of the window panes were cracked or were missing completely, so only the iron frame remained. This hall might once have welcomed guests with some degree of warmth and charm, but those days were long gone. An icy draught blew through the broken window, and the floor was covered with bird droppings. And I mean totally covered. You couldn't even see what colour it had been originally, nor whether it was a tiled or a wooden floor. There were bird droppings on the walls, bird droppings on the steps and the banister, bird droppings everywhere.

Now all that bird poo had to come from somewhere. I peered up nervously at the staircase in the twilight. Nothing moved, which was probably why it took me so long to spot them, but they were there – on the railings and the banister and the cross beams, all the way up through the dim stairwell, up to the rafters right under the roof. I could see that they were birds, but not what kind. They were resting with their heads tucked under one wing and their grey feathers puffed up so they resembled big dust bunnies.

"Are those your sisters?" I whispered to The Nothing.

"Yes. But you don't have to whisper. They don't mind noise." The Nothing flapped her wings furiously and managed to elevate herself almost two metres. "Heelloo!" she yelled. "Heeeellllooooouuuuuuoooooouuuuu..."

I jumped, but the sisters didn't even twitch a feather.

"Are they... hibernating or something?" I asked.

"I don't know what that means," said The Nothing.

"I mean, do they sleep during the winter?"

"Oh, I see. No. No, I don't think so. They're just waiting."

"What for?"

"I don't know. But they're not asleep. Not really."

I took one cautious step forwards, keeping my eyes fixed on the vast, motionless flock of sisters. Nothing happened, so I took another one. I closed my eyes for a split second in order to get a better sense of where Oscar's thread was leading me – upstairs, it seemed. And now I thought I could hear muted voices coming from the same direction. Still keeping half an eye on the sisters, I tiptoed up the stairs to the first landing, which ran the width of the room like a sort of gallery. There was a door at each end, but I stopped in front of a set of tall double doors in the centre and pressed my ear against the woodwork. No one was saying anything now, but the voices had come from in there, I was sure of it. I knelt down and tried to peer through the keyhole.

"What are you doing?" said The Nothing right behind me, and nearly gave me my second heart attack of the day.

"Shhhhh," I hissed.

Fortunately, she didn't respond with: "What does that mean?" She just pressed her lips together and nodded eagerly.

I couldn't see much apart from a big patch of faded carpet. A table leg, something which might be a lamp... and a foot.

That foot belonged to Oscar. I would have recognized those hi-tops anywhere.

I tried the handle – it wasn't locked – and opened the door.

It was an old-fashioned sort of parlour, with furniture upholstered in moss-like green velvet, fringed lampshades, logs burning in the fireplace, and mahogany bookcases with glass doors. The first thing I really looked at, though, was Oscar. And he in turn stared at me and at The Nothing who came flapping inside at my heels.

"Duuuuuuuuuuck!" he screamed at the top of his voice and dived behind the armchair he had been lounging in.

Woofer yelped fearfully and tried squashing himself under the sofa. Bumble barked loudly, Aunt Isa brandished an old umbrella rather like a sword, and looked unusually confrontational. Only Shanaia, who was lying on the sofa, showed no reaction at all.

"It's only me..." I said. But it wasn't me they were staring at. It was The Nothing.

"It's not like them," Aunt Isa said, lowering her brolly. "I don't know what it is, but it isn't one of them. Clara, close the door."

Aunt Isa had a large, bloody wound on her temple and blood in her hair; one shoulder was bloodstained and torn. Hoot-Hoot was perched on one of the bookcases, looking unusually ruffled. And when Oscar slowly emerged from his hiding place behind the armchair, I could see that he too had the same kind of bloody gouges on his forearms.

"What happened?" I asked.

"Shut that door *now*!" Aunt Isa snapped, and I did as I was told.

"Are they still out there?" Oscar wanted to know.

"Who? What are you talking about?"

"Those... shark birds."

"What?"

"I think he means my sisters," The Nothing said helpfully. "The ones that turned out right..."

CHAPTER 17

Chimera's Voice

"They're *totally* creepy," Oscar said. "They look like birds, but... they have these jaws. You know, like a shark. Full of *teeth*..." He raised one injured arm. The skin had been ripped off in a circle the size of a tennis ball. "It really hurts. They sink their fangs into you and refuse to let go and... and they keep biting until you kill them. There are hundreds of them. They sit there just waiting for you."

"But... they didn't do anything to me when I came up the stairs."

"Nope, but just wait until you try to escape."

"It's a trap," Shanaia said out of the blue; she was still lying on the sofa, staring into the air, looking as if she'd stopped caring about everything. "The whole thing is a trap, and it's all my fault..."

Aunt Isa looked as if she felt sorry for her, but she didn't say "no, of course it isn't" or words to that effect.

"You couldn't know," Oscar said. "You didn't do it on purpose..."

"What are you talking about?" I asked. "She couldn't know what?"

"She wants to capture you," Shanaia said. "I knew that all along, but I... all I could think about was Westmark. And somehow I got it into my head that you were the only one who could help me get Westmark back."

"Not 'somehow'," Aunt Isa said. "It was Chimera. Chimera did everything in her power to convince you. And she didn't let you escape until she was sure that you truly believed it."

"I should have known it was all too easy," Shanaia said bitterly. "Chimera never lets her prey get away before she's done with it..."

I caught myself rubbing Cat's scratches between my eyebrows. Possibly because right now I felt a bit like prey myself.

"Are you saying... that you didn't get away? That she deliberately let you go?"

"I thought I'd made my own escape. But she was just using me the way a hunter uses a bird dog to flush out his target," Shanaia said in a low voice. "Only this dog wasn't good enough. I couldn't persuade you to come with me to Westmark. So instead she took Oscar and Woofer and used them as bait. And then... and then..." She gasped for air a couple of times, as if it physically hurt her to say the words, "then I betrayed my friends."

"Shanaia..."Aunt Isa held up a hand as if to stop the bitter flow of self-recrimination.

"No. It's the truth. That's what I did. *You* would never have... she would never have been able to... if it hadn't been for me."

"She'd captured your wildfriend," Aunt Isa said. "Of course you would come to her."

"I shouldn't have done it."

"If it had been Hoot-Hoot..."Aunt Isa said. "I would have done the same thing."

"No, you wouldn't. You're wiser and stronger. You don't betray people. You don't tell... tell people where your friends are most vulnerable. How best to trick them." Her gaze fell on Oscar.

"So it was you who..." I didn't quite know how to finish the sentence. "Did you tell Chimera that Oscar and I..."

Shanaia nodded in anguish. "But..." Her voice almost faded away. "But... she killed Elfrida anyway. As a punishment. Because I'd been a bad dog."

Elfrida. That had been the name of the ferret. I remembered the stiff little body in the cardboard box back at Aunt Isa's. Poor Elfrida. Poor Shanaia.

She'd sat up now and pulled her knees right up to her chest. It made her look both smaller and younger. Once upon a time I'd actually wondered if Shanaia might be right and Chimera really was frightened of me for some reason. But of course, that had never been the case. The feeble hope curled up inside me and died. Chimera had never been afraid of me. That wasn't why she had kept her distance. She'd known all along that by picking the right bait and not interfering, she would have stupid Clara walk straight into her trap like a good little girl.

"I was so hoping that you wouldn't come," Shanaia said. "And then you came anyway."

"Yes." Then I remembered something. "Were you the one saying 'go away'?"

"What do you mean?"

"There was a kestrel..." I told them about it, and the voices The Nothing could hear.

"I don't know," Shanaia said. "I... was only wishing."

"Perhaps that was enough," Aunt Isa said. "You're part of Westmark. When you wish for something hard enough, all of Westmark can feel it."

Shanaia lowered her head. "It doesn't matter now," she said. "Because it didn't make any difference."

So now only one big question remained.

"Why?" I asked. "What does she want with me?"

"Read the book," Chimera said.

My heart stopped. It truly did. It started again, but it had stopped for one panicky moment. I looked around like a maniac, but I couldn't see anyone other than us – Oscar, Aunt Isa, Shanaia and me. No bird woman with giant wings.

And yet it had been her voice. I was certain.

"Where are you?" Aunt Isa said. "Chimera, you're breaking the law. Let us go."

I didn't think that Aunt Isa believed for one minute that Chimera cared about the law any more. She just wanted her to speak again, so we could determine which direction her voice was coming from.

"Read the book. Then I'll let you go."

I turned around and stared at The Nothing. She was perched on the armrest of the easy chair, digging her fingerfeet into the fabric to stay upright. Her eyes looked completely vacant.

"What book?" I asked, to be quite sure about the voice.

"The Nothing knows," Chimera's voice said, but it was coming out of The Nothing's mouth. "Find it and read it. But hurry up. The sisters are getting hungry."

"Chimera," Aunt Isa said with an icy rage that instinctively made me duck. "Release that poor creature and speak for yourself."

The Nothing blinked.

"What...?" she said and sneezed violently. "I'b so bery, bery sorry..." she mumbled and went cross-eyed for a moment, then she fell off the armrest and landed on the floor with a feathery bump, all floppy and unconscious.

The Nothing was lying on her back on the rug with her fingerfeet up in the air and her eyes closed. Oscar peered at her suspiciously.

"What *is* that thing?" he asked. "And why did its voice suddenly change?"

"She's some sort of failed experiment," I said and surprised myself at how angry I sounded. "A chimera who didn't turn out quite the way Chimera wanted. Chimera put her in a cage and abandoned her because she got fed up with The Nothing following her."

"The Nothing?"

"It's what she calls it." I corrected myself. "Her. She's a her, not an it. A *person*, not a thing. Or a nothing, for that matter."

"But Chimera can talk through her," Aunt Isa said pensively. "That must mean she used some part of herself when she created her."

"Excuse me," Shanaia interjected, "but shouldn't we be more interested in *what* she said, rather than *how* she said it?"

"And you're not suggesting that Chimera is going to let us all walk out of here if we just read some book aloud to her, are you?" Oscar said.

"Books can be important to a wildwitch," Aunt Isa replied. "And possibly even more to someone who is now a... different kind of witch. Like Chimera."

"You may be right, but surely she can do her own reading and writing?"

"Yes."

"Then why make such a fuss about a book that's been sitting on a shelf here – for years possibly?" Oscar looked sceptical.

"There has to be more to it," Aunt Isa conceded. "Shanaia, are there any... special books in this house?"

"Grimoires, black books and necronomicons? Isa, you should know better. You know us." Shanaia's facial expression changed abruptly. "Or you used to know us. I'm the only one left now. But with the exception of my great-grandfather Shaemas, who was a bit of an oddball, we've never dabbled in that kind of thing: the dark arts, blood magic and all that. We're wildwitches, pure and simple. Or rather, we were."

There was something terribly lost and lonely about Shanaia. I remember being a bit scared the first time I met her – her dyed hair, the ink-black make-up around her eyes, the studs, and not least

Elfrida, who hadn't exactly been the cutest and cuddliest of wildfriends. But maybe the point of all that wildness and the Goth attitude was to help Shanaia convince herself that she was tough, that she didn't need anyone. Right now she looked neither wild nor dangerous, just very, very alone.

"What really happened to your parents?" I asked.

"They died," was all she said.

It was obvious that she would rather not talk about it. But what if it had something to do with all of this – Westmark, Chimera, that mysterious book she was so keen to get her claws on?

"They were going to a Walpurgis Night gathering at Raven Kettle," Aunt Isa said. "Shanaia was only four years old, too young to go with them. In fact, I was her babysitter myself that night. We don't know exactly what happened, only that... somehow they must have got lost on the wildways. It took us five days to find them and by then it was too late." She looked at me, her eyes filled with shadows. "If you lose your way, it's not only hunger and thirst that can kill you. The wildways fog itself will consume a little of your life force with every passing hour, especially if you don't know where you're going. Eventually... you just lie down and die. At least Shanaia's parents had each other. They lay down together, embraced each other, and that was how they died."

"So it wasn't because... someone killed them?"

"No."

"I thought perhaps... perhaps Chimera had done it..."

"No," Aunt Isa said. "There's nothing to suggest that. Chimera didn't appear until later."

"Chimera didn't appear until she saw a chance to steal Westmark," Shanaia said darkly.

"How did she do that?" Oscar asked.

"When my parents died, my Aunt Abbie looked after me. Or... she wasn't *my* aunt, but rather my mum's. So I guess that makes her a great-aunt or something, but I never called her anything other than Aunt Abbie. She was quite old and eccentric, and lots of people said she wasn't a suitable person to bring up a child, but... but I loved her. She was my mum and my dad and my best friend. She wasn't exactly the domestic type, and people used to gossip about the house being messy... but then again we spent most of our days outside and we ate things that we found, and lit fires in the garden and on the beach, and boiled mussels, and... she taught me *everything*. Everything about Westmark. And when we came home in the evening, she always gave me a bath. The house might have been a bit dirty, but I wasn't. And she would read to me, and we would draw pictures of the things we'd seen that day, and... and... I thought it would last forever. Of course I knew that she was old, but she was as strong as an ox and almost as quick on her feet as I was. I mean, the woman climbed trees, for Pete's sake. She and I would sit in the cherry tree, eating cherries, spitting out the stones and..." Shanaia's face contorted. "How was I to know that one day she would suddenly sit down in a chair and die? But she did. Without warning me, without saying anything, just like that... bang." She stared at us defiantly. "I miss her more than I miss my parents. She looked after me for ten years. She would never have sold Westmark without first discussing it with me. She would never have sold Westmark at all."

"But... is that what she did?" I said.

"No, I keep telling you. It was a trick."

"Chimera produced a sales contract, which Abigael had signed," Aunt Isa said. "Or at least so it appeared. It became effective on Abigael's death, and there was a lot of waffle about 'providing for the child's education and offering her financial security' and blah blah. Enough so that it could be argued that Abigael had simply wanted to do what was best for Shanaia the day she was no longer around to care for her herself."

"But Aunt Abbie would never have agreed that leaving Westmark was 'in my best interest'," Shanaia said. "She would never have sent me to that ridiculously expensive boarding school. How could anyone think so?"

"The Raven Mothers thought so," Aunt Isa said. "They decided that the sale was valid, and that Shanaia would leave Westmark and start at Oakhurst Academy. An exclusive boarding school favoured by some wildwitch families."

"It's a *horrible* place," Shanaia said. "You're trapped inside a classroom most of the day, and I wasn't allowed to have Elfrida with me during term. I ran away after three weeks..."

"And the school kept the money..."Aunt Isa said. "They said it wasn't their fault that Shanaia 'refused to let herself be taught'."

"... and then you had no aunt and no home and no money," Oscar said. "That's messed up."

"All I had was Elfrida," Shanaia said, and at this point her eyes looked practically extinguished. Because now she had lost Elfrida too.

The whole story was so sad I could hardly bear it.

"We have to do something," I said. "We can't just sit here feeling glum. Is there really no way past those shark birds?"

"I'm not risking it again," Oscar said, picking at one of his cuts.

"But..." I thought about the seagulls and the wild dogs. "... What if they don't hurt *me*?"

"Why wouldn't they hurt you?" Oscar said. "I don't think they're fussy. They'll eat anything."

"Yes, but..." I started explaining what had happened with the wild dogs. Or rather, what hadn't happened. "It felt as if they didn't want to... draw blood."

Aunt Isa scrutinized me.

"There has to be something about you," she said at length. "Given the lengths Chimera went to to bring you here. If it's at all possible – then make your escape. Get out of here. Seek out the Raven Mothers and tell them that we're here, and that... that they have to do something. Chimera is more than just a wildwitch who has crossed the line. When I see what she has done here, soul-stripping animals and creating chimeras and..." She looked down at the still unconscious Nothing. "We have to stop her. Otherwise it won't only be Westmark that's in danger, but all of the wildworld. Tell them that!"

"And hurry up," Oscar said a tad nervously. "Don't forget she said something about the shark birds getting hungry..."

CHAPTER 18

Guard Dog

"Are you quite sure?" Aunt Isa asked. "It goes without saying that we'll help you if you're wrong, and they attack you. But it could be dangerous."

"We're already in danger," I said. "Waiting here in the drawing room might *feel* less dangerous, but it really isn't." How I wished that Cat were here, then I would feel a lot less scared. Cat was always so good at making me feel brave.

Aunt Isa smiled to me in a very Aunt Isa way. She cupped my face in her hands and gave me a quick peck on my forehead.

"You're growing, Clara," she said. "It's good to see."

Oscar, too, looked a little surprised at my volunteering, but for once he kept his mouth shut.

I took a deep breath. I felt as if I should be running on the spot or doing some push-ups. I mean, that's what you do before a major sports challenge isn't it, warm up? And this was much more difficult.

I opened the door to the landing. It was quiet outside, just as before, but possibly a little darker. Perhaps it had clouded over outside. Or maybe it was all in my mind. I could sense the sisters more than I could see them. This still, motionless waiting that wasn't sleep.

You walked past them less than an hour ago, I reminded myself. They didn't even twitch. You can walk past them now. Remember the seagulls. Remember the wild dogs – especially Lop-Ear. For whatever reason they will leave you alone, or... at least they won't bite you.

I started walking. I could have run, but I decided against it – if you're tiptoeing past a guard dog, it's a really bad idea to start running because it'll chase you just by instinct. So I walked, one step, two steps towards the stairs.

I thought I heard a flutter. I looked up. A few of the nearest sisters stretched their wings and, for the first time, I could see their heads.

Perhaps it was just as well that I hadn't seen them earlier because I'm not sure I would have dared venture outside. They had no beaks – to that extent they bore a slight resemblance to The Nothing. But instead of a lost little girl's face, there was... practically nothing but a huge mouth. The eyes were reduced to shiny pinheads in the feathers, and just like Oscar had said, they had shark jaws bursting with sharp, triangular teeth, not just one row, but two or three.

I stopped in my tracks. I didn't mean to. I really didn't mean to.

Come on, I told myself. Onwards. OK, so they're looking at you. That won't kill you. Keep moving...

I took a few more steps, but I couldn't help make them a little faster. I'd almost reached the stairs now. I wouldn't say I was running, but neither was I out for a leisurely stroll.

The minute I put my foot on the first step, I heard a huge *whoosh*. I looked up. The whole stairwell had come alive. A swarm of sisters had taken to their wings as if controlled by a single will.

Now I ran. I made a dash for the bottom, but I still only managed a few steps before they were on me.

"*Go away!*" I screamed at the top of my wild-witch voice. "**GO *AWAY*!**"

I flailed my arms about as I ran, and I did hit some of them, but there were just so *many* of them. Thud. Thud. Thud. They hit my back and my head, my shoulders and my chest, my arms and my legs like feathery rubber bullets.

It was horrible, but I quickly realized that they weren't actually sinking their teeth into me. In that way they *did* act just like the wild dogs and the seagulls. As long as I could keep going long enough to reach the front door, as long as I could make it outside...

I forced myself to carry on. I stopped lashing out at them, except when they aimed themselves directly at my face. But the strikes continued and they began attaching themselves to me with their claws. My body grew heavier and heavier, and my foot caught on the edge of a step because I failed to raise it high enough. Losing my balance, I made a desperate grab for the banister, but my arms weighed much more than they usually did. I was half turned around by the weight on my back and I fell, tumbling and landing not on the hard stairs, but on top of hundreds of soft bodies. Some of them were squashed; I heard the sound of delicate, light bones snapping like twigs and felt a wet warmth against my hip. It didn't hurt. It wasn't my blood. But the weight on top of me doubled abruptly.

I'm going to suffocate, I thought, and started bashing them again with my heavy arms, kicking them with my heavy legs, twisting my heavy body. I made it halfway to my feet, but fell back again, fighting to keep from being submerged in a flood of feathered bodies...

"Clara!" It was Oscar calling out to me, I thought, but he sounded much further away than he really was.

"Turn back!" Aunt Isa's voice cut through the whirr of wings. "Clara, you can't do it. Come back here!" Then a shrill, ear-piercing note rang out, a wildsong, but a form of wildsong I'd never heard before – a war cry that was an attack in itself. It seemed to pierce the mass of feathered bodies, and the weight on me eased a little. I managed to scramble to my feet and reach the banister. Clinging to it for dear life, I hauled myself up a step or two, when suddenly a hand grabbed mine. I batted a sister wing away from my face and could see that the hand belonged to Shanaia. She was dragging me back up the stairs while her wildsong keening grew louder and louder, and I couldn't believe how all that sound could come out of just one girl. Aunt Isa had started singing too, and I could see both her and Oscar beating off the sisters, not with their bare hands, but with heavy books they used almost as if they were baseball bats and the sister birds were balls. With Shanaia's help I made it back onto the landing, and when Aunt Isa got hold of my other arm, I was able to stagger the last few paces back into the drawing room.

Hoot-Hoot only just made it inside before Oscar slammed the door shut. Hoot-Hoot had fought too, I could see. He had blood on his beak and on one wing. Shanaia grabbed a book and slammed it down on the head of one of the sister birds that had chased after us; Aunt Isa brutally tore a couple more out of my hair and off my back, and wrung their necks as if they were chickens for the dinner plate.

Aunt Isa, Oscar and Shanaia were all bleeding from fresh injuries. Shanaia's were the worst, one shoulder looked like someone had tried to push it through a shredder. Her leather jacket was in tatters, and her naked, bloody shoulder stuck out through the lining. There was hardly any skin left. In one place, something blue and sinewy could be glimpsed in the depths of the raw redness of the gash. Shanaia hadn't guarded herself at all, she had fought simply to save me.

I was the only person without a scratch and I felt weirdly guilty about it. I had been congratulating myself for trying to save them, but instead they'd ended up coming to my rescue and paid for it with cuts and blood and pain.

"I'm sorry," I said, although strictly speaking I hadn't done anything wrong.

"It was worth a try," was all Aunt Isa said, and placed her hands on Shanaia's shoulders. The wild-song returned, this time the calm, humming sing-song so much more familiar to me than Shanaia's wild battle cry, and it looked as if it was stemming the bleeding a little. Shanaia was deathly pale, and her black-rimmed eyes looked like cinders in her white face.

"It's no good," Oscar panted, sucking his wrist, which had acquired yet another shark bird bite. "We can't get out that way."

"Can't we use the wildways?" I asked.

Aunt Isa shook her head. "Few wildwitches can find the wildways indoors," she said. "Most of us need the sky above our heads and grass, soil or rock under our feet."

Cat could do it, I thought. But then again, he needed only a hole in the fog big enough for him to

136

slip through – a kind of sophisticated cat flap. Besides, I was starting to realize that Cat didn't really think most of the laws of the universe applied to him.

Aunt Isa sang another wildsong for Shanaia's shoulder. And another one.

"We haven't even got water," she said. "Oscar, check the drinks cabinet to see if there's anything other than mediocre sherry. Vodka or schnapps would be the best."

"Aunt Abbie preferred brandy," Shanaia said in a croaky voice. "I don't think she was much of a vodka drinker."

"Why is that so important?" I asked.

"The wound is quite deep," Aunt Isa explained. "Even with wildsong... it would be good to get it cleaned up. And vodka is almost pure alcohol."

"There's nothing like that," said Oscar, who had opened a rather large mahogany cabinet that was clearly not, after all, the innocent bookshelf it had first appeared to be. "But there is some whisky. Will that do?"

"I guess it's better than nothing," Aunt Isa said.

Oscar brought the bottle, and Aunt Isa carefully tipped a little of the whisky into Shanaia's cut.

Shanaia inhaled sharply. It clearly stung.

"I'm sorry, sweetheart," Aunt Isa said quietly. "But..."

"I know," Shanaia said through clenched teeth. "I know."

However, the strange thing was that despite her injuries and the pain, she looked better than she had when I first entered the drawing room. The lost and resigned expression had gone. Her eyes had come alive once more.

"Thank you for saving me," I said. "I wouldn't have made it up the stairs without you."

She didn't exactly smile, but she did nod.

"Hey, what about us?" Oscar said. "We saved you too."

"Yes, of course you did. Thank you so much."

"How very charming," The Nothing suddenly jeered in Chimera's voice. "But I see that you still haven't got the message."

We turned as one to The Nothing, still lying on the floor with her legs in the air, but obviously useable as Chimera's mouthpiece all the same. At that moment there was a loud crash from one of the three tall windows in the drawing room. I only caught a brief glimpse of a large, white body, then it was gone and only a bloody imprint remained on the window pane. Then the next seagull attacked. Another crash. And the next. It wasn't until the sixth seagull's attempt that the window shattered and a shower of large and small shards of glass rained down on the rug.

The seagulls made no attempt to get inside. Their mission seemed purely to break the glass. And they didn't stop until all three windows lay shattered on the floor and the winter wind howled through the bloodstained, jagged holes.

"You have one hour to find my book," Chimera's voice said. "Then the sisters will come for you."

CHAPTER 19

The Blank Book

"Chimera!" Aunt Isa said in a very loud voice. "How much is that book worth to you?"

A pause followed. I don't think Chimera had intended for The Nothing to act as a communications channel, merely a link in the chain of command. She would speak, we would obey. That was more what she'd had in mind.

"We don't know which book you're talking about," Aunt Isa then said and picked a random volume from the bookcase. "Could it be this one?"

Chimera still made no reply, but The Nothing sat up with a jerk, possibly so that Chimera could borrow her eyes just like the Raven Mothers would borrow those of the ravens. Aunt Isa flicked indifferently through the book.

"Hmmm," she said. "It doesn't look all that interesting. I guess it's not the one." She tossed it into the flames in the fireplace, which flattened at first from the air pressure and then shot up again, taller than before. She took another book.

"So what about this one? Yes? No? Don't know?" She did the same thing again – leafing through it before tossing it onto the flames – and then reached for a third book.

"Wait!" The Nothing croaked in Chimera's voice. "Wait..."

"What does it look like?" Aunt Isa said. "Is it green – like this one?" She chucked yet another book onto the flames.

I just watched with my mouth hanging open. What was my aunt doing? Didn't she realize that the only person who could get us out of this trap was Chimera? Did she really think it was a smart move to make her even angrier than she already was?

"Or red?"

"Brown," The Nothing said, and this time she sounded more like herself. "It's brown with a kind of wheel on the spine and on the cover..." She pointed with her wing. "It's somewhere on that bookcase."

Oscar jumped up and immediately began pulling all the brown books off the shelves to see if one featured a wheel. If it didn't, it ended up on the floor with a crash. Within fifteen to twenty seconds, there was almost the same number of discarded books at his feet, but he carried on until there were no more brown books left in the bookcase.

"It's not here," he said at length. "There are books about birds and mushrooms and fairy tales and stars, but not one of them has a wheel on its spine or on its cover."

"Let the witch child look," Chimera's voice said irritably. "If she can't find it, you're all as useless as that ball of feathers."

"Why is that book so important to you?" Aunt Isa asked, more quietly now that Chimera had started listening and responding.

"That's none of your business, Isa. It's important because you can save your lives by finding it and reading it to me. That's why."

I had squatted down next to the messy pile of books on the floor. Oscar was right. Books about birds, mushrooms...

No. Wait. Wasn't that...

Yes. A brown book with something which, with a bit of goodwill, could be a wheel or at least a circle with a kind of cross inside it.

"Is this it?" I asked, holding it up.

"What does it say inside?" Chimera asked.

I opened it and was just about to start reading, but Aunt Isa stopped me.

"Wait," she said. "I'm not at all sure that we should tell Chimera what it says."

"Would you rather die, Isa? Would you rather see your three little apprentices die? It would take less than half an hour before there would be nothing but a few scraps of flesh left on their bones. Would you like to see the bones of the witch child? I can tell the sisters to save you for last, so you don't miss anything."

It was mind-boggling to hear such threats come out of the mouth of a clumsy, sneezing little feather duster like The Nothing. In contrast to her sisters out on the landing it was quite hard to be scared of her. It should have followed that anything she said would be equally unfrightening, but it wasn't. On the contrary. I could feel the hairs stand up at the back of my neck. And just about everywhere else, to be honest.

I was still holding the book. It wasn't a big, heavy book like a bible or an encyclopedia, more a kind of notebook, bound in cracked time-worn leather. Old. Proper old. Somehow I could feel it.

"If you don't want me to read it..." I began, but Aunt Isa stopped me with a gesture.

"Why should we trust you?" she challenged Chimera. "You're an outlaw. You have no honour. And you've tricked us before. How do we know that you'll keep your word this time? If I'm going to die anyway, I would rather feed the book to the fire and know that at least I thwarted your plan."

"You're such a goody two shoes, Isa," Chimera said. "Always so prim and proper, always so righteous. Don't you ever yearn for more? Are you really happy living in a crumbling shack in the middle of nowhere, spending all your time treating lice-infested hedgehogs and crook-winged sparrows?"

"Yes," said Aunt Isa simply. "I live just the way I want to."

"Is that all you want?" Chimera snarled. "Is that really all you want? Still, if it makes you happy, it's no skin off my nose. You may go back to your insignificant little life. And take your hangers-on with you."

"Do you swear?" Aunt Isa said. "Do you swear by blood and by life, by cunning and by caprice, by strength and by seed? Do you swear by everything you are, everything you have been, and everything you will be? *Do you swear?*"

There was a touch of wildsong in those words, and I suddenly understood that Aunt Isa was demanding more than a promise. It was a pledge. A pledge in which the spoken words bound the speaker's will so that she really couldn't break her promise, even if she tried.

"You think you're oh-so clever, eh?" said The Nothing in Chimera's voice. Aunt Isa made no reply. She merely took the book from my hands and held it over the flames.

"Very well," Chimera said. "If it means so much to you. When you have fulfilled your part of the deal and everything has been revealed, I swear that everyone in this room is free to leave and that nothing here will harm you. This I swear, by blood and by life, by cunning and by caprice, by strength and by seed, by everything I am, everything I have been, and everything I will be. Make it so!"

As the last word sounded, it was as if the air thickened for a moment and it grew harder to breathe. The flames flickered, and The Nothing collapsed, close to fainting for a second time.

"Help," she said in a very small voice, now entirely her own. "I think... I think my head is going to crack open."

Aunt Isa listened for a while. Long enough for Oscar to start twitching nervously.

"Was that it?" he then said. "I'm not saying it didn't sound cool, but..."

"She can't go back on that promise," Aunt Isa declared. "Not if she wants to go on living." She turned away from the fireplace and opened the book.

"What does it say?" Oscar asked.

Aunt Isa furrowed her brow. "Nothing special," she said. "Shanaia, is this your Aunt Abbie's handwriting?"

"Yes. That's her notebook, or one of them, at any rate. She would always write down when the swallows arrived, where to find chanterelles or how much sugar to add to her blueberry jam. Stuff like that... A lot of the old books on the shelves are blank, either because the ink has faded away, or because nothing was ever written inside them... This must be one of them."

"How odd," Aunt Isa said. "I find it hard to believe that Chimera would set all this in motion simply to get your aunt's recipe for blueberry jam..."

"Please may I see it?" I asked.

She handed me the book.

"For one kilo of blueberries you will need one kilo of sugar," it said in a slanted and somewhat straggling hand which had to be Aunt Abbie's. "You may want to add a little redcurrant juice and a pinch of black pepper, it gives bite and depth to the taste..."

But that wasn't all of it.

"It says something else," I said. "Behind it. Underneath it... Look!"

"Where?" Aunt Isa said.

"There." There was another hand, fainter, but the more I looked at it, the clearer it became. I couldn't understand how Aunt Isa hadn't spotted what I had seen immediately.

"I can see nothing but blueberry jam," she said. "Shanaia? Can you?"

Shanaia hobbled towards us – her shoulder would not appear to be her only injury. She glanced over my shoulder, at her aunt's directions. And only at them.

"I can't see anything," she said. "Nothing except Aunt Abbie's handwriting."

"But it's right there," I insisted, double-checking to be sure. I turned the page to see if it continued. It did – more clearly. It was difficult to read because the letters were a little different from the ones I was used to, but they spelled out something.

"Read it aloud," Aunt Isa said. "If you can..."

I held the book so that the glow from the fire fell on the page. And, as soon as I saw the first three desperate words, it was as if the room around me became unreal, and only the words on the page mattered. I read...

CHAPTER 20

Oblivion

I am Viridian. I need to write this down. If I do not, soon I will barely be able to remember it myself. I must write it down and read it every day. Every single day. Then I will remember.

I am Viridian. That is my name, that is who I am. Daughter of Aurora, wife of Biarnis, mother of Mino and Ellis. A wildwitch. A woman. Someone. I exist. I am here. I am not yet dead.

When I came to after the battle, I thought that I had won. The rocks were silent, the wheel no longer glowed. I was alive and the Bloodling had gone. Surely I must have been victorious?

I had lost too much blood. I could see it in the sand, the rocks and the wellspring – they had soaked up such copious gore, and yet had choked on these final thick shiny ribbons of blood, like a sponge unable to absorb any more. I could feel it, too, in my galloping heart and the thirst tearing at my throat and screaming from every pore of my body. Blessed Powers, what I wouldn't give to be rid of this thirst – yet I knew that I was lucky to feel anything at all.

Blood. So much of this is about blood. My blood lives on in my heirs, Bravita has none. This, or so I thought, was my victory, even if the wounds she had inflicted on me were to prove to be mortal. Whether I lived or died, my blood would flow on in the veins of my sons, and my memory would live on in their hearts.

False was that hope, and foolish was I to harbour it.

I am Viridian. That is my name, that is who I am. Remember me. Remember!

Nightclaw lay by my side, he too had survived. I buried my fingers in his fur and rested my aching head against his flank.

Up, he said. Get up. Whoever stays down, dies first.

He was right. But my strength was spent; only my will remained, and even that was weak. I could feel it slipping away from me; I was starting to forget why it was important to get up.

Nightclaw sank a talon into my hand. *Up. Up-up-up!*

Oh, Blessed Powers. My weakness gored me with a claw much sharper than his, but in the end I got to my feet. He has always been very good at getting his way.

The wind whistled through the hidden cracks and passages of the cave. The tremors had died down, and the bedrock was still under my feet, almost as if it had never bucked and kicked under our feet, trying to throw us off. But the dust still lingered in the air, and now and then I could hear something clatter and fall somewhere in the subterranean dark.

I would not be able to use the old steps, I realized that after just a few paces. Too much of the ceiling had caved in, and I no longer had the strength to dig my way to freedom. There was only one way out and that was to follow the trickle of the wellspring, through the passage it had carved to reach the sea.

Before I set off on my long and difficult journey, I looked around the cave one last time. There was not much light now – what little daylight that crept through the cracks was dwindling, and night was likely to fall outside soon. But I could still see the wheel carved into the floor of the grotto. It was as still and silent as the bedrock now, still but intact. It had not been broken. Westmark had yet to fall.

I was just about to turn away when I saw it.

An impurity, a flaw. Not in the hub or in the wheel's rim, but in the quarter of the circle that belonged to Westmark and me. I threw myself down on my knees, without thought for the difficulties standing up again would present. My own blood was spilt across that part of the circle, but that shouldn't matter, it belonged there, I was as much a part of Westmark as Westmark was a part of me. But underneath it... I tore off my kerchief and wiped away my clotting blood as best I could. The rock looked different now, no longer a part of the bedrock of the cave. Like sand melting in extreme heat, the rock had melted and then hardened as clear as quartz or glass. And underneath the surface, I saw my enemy. Her upturned face staring right into mine, her hands reaching up towards me, and on the underside of the quartz she had written, not with my blood, but with her own, the curse that was already starting to affect me. Only one symbol – the symbol for oblivion. And suddenly

I heard her voice inside me, though her frozen lips never moved:

"No man, no woman, no child. No animal. No thing will remember you. All you did will be undone, all you have said will be unsaid, all you wrote will fade. It matters not to me whether you live or die. For you will be forgotten, forgotten, forgotten, and oblivion will own you for ever."

I barely know how I made it home. At times I wish I had not. Then I would not have seen oblivion in the eyes of my children, then I would not have lived long enough to realize how fragile memory is.

I am Viridian. I am still here. Finally I understand why people raise stones and write books. That they want to be remembered when they are no longer here is easy to understand. But that is not the only reason. For we may be forgotten even while we are still alive — still breathing, thinking, dreaming, speaking. Those of my blood remembered me the longest, but even their memories of me are starting to fade. They look at my clothes as if they cannot remember whose they are. They wonder why doors I have opened are no longer closed. They have stopped seeing me. It is as if their gazes bend around me, as if even the light ignores me. My elder son has forgotten me completely. My younger remembers me only in his dreams, and then he weeps as if I were dead. They can no longer hear my voice. I have tried penning letters, but they seem not to see the writing on the paper.

I am Viridian. I am still here. But only Nightclaw can see me now, and that is not enough. One cannot live nor die like this. Soon, even I will no longer remember who I am.

You have had your revenge, Bravita.

CHAPTER 21

The Wheel

I could barely see the letters towards the end, but not because they were fading.

"Are you crying?" said The Nothing. "Please don't. It makes her angry. I'm not allowed to cry, but I can't help it. I try and I try, but I can't stop myself. It gets worse when I sneeze, and when I feel sad. But I'm always crying a little."

"I'm not crying," I insisted. "I just have... tears in my eyes."

"Why?"

"Because... it must be awful if the people you love can't see you any more. That they've forgotten you even exist."

"Yes," was all she said.

Aunt Isa stared at the pages in the book.

"I still can't see anything," she said. "I heard what you read out loud, but..." She got up abruptly. "Go away," she said, pressing her fingertips against her forehead. "I want to be allowed to remember!"

Then she grabbed a handful of soil from one of the dead pot plants and sprinkled it carefully on the dusty copper plate which protected the floor against sparks flying from the fireplace.

"What are you doing?" Oscar was intrigued.

"Fighting back," she said through gritted teeth. "I've absolutely no intention of letting some four-hundred-year-old ghost decide what I can or can't remember. I want this curse out of my head, and I want it now. Fire..." She looked around. If there had been any candles in the old candlesticks, the mice would have eaten them long ago. Instead she raked one of the glowing coals out of the fireplace with a poker. "This will have to do," she muttered, and prodded it until it lay beside the pile of earth. "Air..." she looked at The Nothing. "Please may we borrow a feather from you?" she asked.

The Nothing looked surprised.

"You want something from me?" She was simultaneously taken aback and proud at the thought and immediately reached up an awkward fingerfoot to pluck a feather from her chest. "Here you go! Is one enough? You're welcome to another one. Or several. I mean..." She sneezed and pooed on the rug. "Whatever you need. I so want to be useful!"

"Thank you," Aunt Isa said in an unusually soft tone of voice. "One will do. You're a great help."

The Nothing looked several inches taller and sneezed happily.

Aunt Isa spat on her forefinger and dipped it in the ashes in the fireplace. Then she carefully drew a cross with four lines exactly the same length and then a large circle around the cross and a tiny circle in the centre. A wheel. A wheel with four spokes that divided it into four quarters. Just like the wheel embossed into the leather of the book. In each of the three quarters now lay the soil, the coal and the feather. She spat again so that the last quarter circle now contained a little bit of water.

"The hub..." she mumbled. "If this is going to work, then..." She looked up at me. I had followed her actions with interest because somehow it was so very unlike Aunt Isa. I had absolutely no doubt that my aunt was a witch, but not *that* kind of witch – not the sort to draw mysterious patterns on the floor and perform complicated rituals. Her witchery was more natural: seeing a little deeper than anyone else, helping nature along with wildsong and herbs, walking the wildways like animals who appear and disappear without your ever seeing how they do it. More sense and instinct than chants and rituals.

"Clara," she said. "I'm afraid I have to ask you for a drop of blood."

"What are you doing?" I said.

"I'm trying to save Vi... Viri... that poor dead woman from oblivion."

"Viridian."

"Yes. Her."

"Can't you even say her name?"

"Not yet," Aunt Isa said grimly. "It takes all my concentration just to remember what I'm trying to do."

"And my blood will help."

"Yes. It will make the hub of the wheel – its centre. It's the hub that gathers together the wheel and makes it complete. Do you understand?"

"Sort of." Though I didn't really. I mean, I could see that that small circle in the middle of the wheel was its centre, but it was harder to understand why it made all the difference.

"The fulcrum," Oscar exclaimed. "Can't you see it, Clara? If it was a real wheel, not just a drawing, then the hub would be the point where the wheel connects to the axle, the point that the whole wheel would revolve around. If a wheel doesn't have a hub, then it isn't a wheel at all, just... eh... a circle."

"OK..." I said slowly. "I guess it kind of makes sense."

"Of course it does," Oscar said. "This will be *so* cool. Come on, Clara, prick your finger or something."

It was Oscar, naturally, who had once thought it a brilliant idea that we should mix blood. Now he looked at me with the same enthusiasm. It really was a shame that it wasn't Oscar who had a wildwitch aunt. He would have loved learning all the stuff that terrified me.

No one had a knife or needle. We ended up using a shard of glass from the broken windows to make a small cut in my ring finger. It stung, the cut ended up being deeper than intended, and my finger started to bleed profusely.

"Hold it over the hub," Aunt Isa said. "And speak Vvv... her name."

Remember Viridian. If ever a message had been drummed into me, I guess it would be that one.

I knelt down beside the wheel and held my finger over the centre. There was no need to squeeze my fingertip to get the blood out, it flowed all by itself, glossy, dark red drops trickling over my fingertip and nail and dropping, almost in slow motion, I thought, onto the black hub of the ash wheel.

The first drops hit it without making a sound. I stared at the blood that slowly filled the whole of the hub without spilling over the lines, forming a perfect blood-red circle. I totally forgot I was meant to say something as well. It was just like when Lop-Ear accidentally pierced the skin on my neck. A part of me was looking at the blood, but at the same time I was still in the blood, I was both inside myself and outside, but more and more outside with each falling drop.

"Clara! Say it!"

Aunt Isa's voice sounded strangely distant. The drops kept falling. I fell with them. The wheel started turning around me. I was at the centre. Everything else was spinning. The fulcrum, Oscar had said, and that was exactly what I was. I stood still. Everything else moved faster and faster until blurred by the speed and then I couldn't see anything. Nothing at all.

CHAPTER 22

"No man, no woman, no child."

When everything stopped spinning, I was in a different place. There was no longer a drawing room, a fireplace or an Aunt Isa. Instead there was darkness and the smell of seaweed and brine, and a few rays of grey daylight falling vertically from small cracks in the roof. Sand. Rock. A distant sound of lapping waves and wind, and seagulls screeching. Water trickling.

This is a dream, I thought. This can't be real.

But it felt incredibly real. I was dizzy. My finger was bleeding. And when I took a wobbly step forwards, everything whirled for a final time, and I had to sit down so as not to fall. The sand was wet under my bottom, and the dampness quickly seeped through my leggings.

There was a sneeze and a farting sound, and someone said:

"I'b so bery, bery sorry."

The Nothing was sitting on her feathered back-side with her tail feathers spread in the sand not far from me.

"I didn't mean to," she said. "Only it's so difficult not to follow someone. I try and I try, but..."

"It's OK," I whispered hoarsely. "I'm glad you're here."

"You are?" she said, and looked completely taken aback.

"Yes." And it was the truth, because her presence made me feel a little less crazy. This had to be real, I hadn't lost my mind and it wasn't a dream. If it had been a dream, I most certainly wouldn't have brought The Nothing along...

The wheel ritual must have gone wrong some-how. Or turned out differently from what Aunt Isa had expected. And here we were, sitting next to each other, The Nothing and I, in an underground cave by the sea.

"Do you think this is the cave that Viridian woman was talking about?" The Nothing asked.

"Yes," I said, because the same thought had crossed my mind. "I don't know why or how we ended up here, but..." Then something else occurred to me.

"Please would you say that again?"

"What?" The Nothing sniffed.

"The name."

"The name?"

"Of the woman from the book," I said patiently.

"Viridian?"

"Yes. You can say it."

"Eh... Yes."

Now that was weird. Shanaia hadn't been able to say it, nor had Aunt Isa, not even Cat could get it out in full no matter how hard he tried. REM EMBERVIR IDI AN and all that. But The Nothing could.

"How is that possible?" I peered closely at the small, snotty-nosed, feathered creature with the constantly weeping eyes. "How can you do that, when nobody else can?" Apart from me, and Chimera, that is, but she didn't count.

"Because I'm The Nothing," she said woefully.

"What do you mean?"

"'No man, no woman, no child. No animal. No thing will remember you'," she quoted. "That was the curse. And I'm the *Nothing*. So I remember. At least some of it. That's why she could use me in the beginning."

"Use you for what?"

"I could see that it said something in the books. But I hadn't learned to read, not to begin with. And when she started teaching me, then... I became a little less Nothing. I became able to do something. I became someone. And then... Then the words faded for me. I mean the words she had written. Viridian. And then I was useless again."

"True," said a voice in the darkness. "You've always been a complete failure in every possible way."

The Nothing's face changed. Her eyes lit up. Her mouth twisted into a blissful smile.

"Mum!!" She squealed ecstatically, and started hopping and flapping across the sand towards Chimera.

CHAPTER 23

Blood Arts

There was barely enough room for her. She held her wings awkwardly, half-folded, and for the first time I wondered what it was like to have them, to live with them every day. Being able to fly would be wonderful, of course, but if the price was that you couldn't get into any place with a ceiling less than four metres high... I'd never thought about that part of it before.

I don't know why I was thinking about it now. Perhaps it was simply to be able to think anything at all, rather than just stare at her in mute panic. My heart was pounding so loud that my ears were popping, and I leapt to my feet so that at least I would be standing when she... when she...

Well, what did I think she was going to do? She'd hunted me for months and made herself an outcast in the wildworld, but I still didn't know what she wanted from me.

Her yellow, predatory eyes rested on me.

"Witch child," she said. "You came. I knew that even Isa Two-Shoes wouldn't be able to resist the temptation."

"Temptation?" I croaked. "What temptation?"

"To lift the curse. But your witch aunt doesn't understand the blood arts as well as she thinks she does."

Blood arts. No one had ever really told me what the term meant, and yet I understood. Something inside me recognized it and knew that it was what happened to me when my blood mixed with something else. It was why I sometimes knew what Oscar was doing even when I wasn't with him. It was the reason I could "talk" to Cat – since that first morning in the stairwell when he had clawed me between the eyes, from the moment he had licked up my blood, we'd been bound to each other. It was blood arts that had freed Lop-Ear from enslavement, and it was blood arts that had brought me into this cave.

Chimera's wings suddenly swept forwards, and I was knocked over. She kept flapping her wings, long, quick, swishing strokes that raised the sand into the air and whirled it around. I had to narrow my eyes to keep it out, it clogged up my nose and crunched between my teeth, I was caught in the middle of a raging sandstorm and I had to spit and spit, half blind and half deaf from the hissing sand and the rush of her wings.

I tried to get up, but a swift wing stroke knocked me back down. I couldn't stand, I couldn't even sit, only lie gasping and dazed in the gritty sand until the storm finally settled around me. It felt a bit as if she'd whacked me in the back of the head with a golf club, but as it turned out, she hadn't just used her wings because she wanted to knock me to the ground.

She had swept away most of the sand from the floor of the cave. Under the sand the ground was completely level and glassy. "... as clear as quartz or glass," Viridian had written in her book, and although the rasping of sand through the centuries had made it less distinct, I could still see the outline of a large crossed wheel, almost identical to the one Aunt Isa had marked out in the drawing room, only ten or twenty times bigger. And I was lying almost exactly in the middle. Somehow that felt ominous, and I tried to crawl away, but my arms and legs wouldn't cooperate.

"Earth," Chimera called out in a voice that grated like metal against rock. From the darkness around us emerged a... a mole? It was one of the biggest I'd ever seen. Or perhaps it only looked bigger because I was lying on the floor. Its pink snout twitched as it crept forwards, its shovel-like front paws slipping clumsily on the smooth floor. This place wasn't right for it. But Chimera gave it no choice. She pointed a long taloned finger at one quarter of the circle, and the mole scrabbled across the floor until it reached the spot she had pointed at. I could see its flanks move in shuddering breaths, and I thought I could sense its fear. It didn't want to be here. This wasn't where it belonged. It wanted to go back to its underground tunnels, to wet soil and the smell of worms, to moist leaves and crunchy beetles and grass roots that lit up the darkness with their juicy scent.

"Water!" Chimera's second command made me jump as if she were summoning me. But she wasn't. It was another creature forcing itself, or being forced, across the floor of the cave, from the corner where the smell of the sea and the cries of seagulls were strongest. A small grey speckled seal, with eyes that reminded me of Woofer's brown labrador gaze. It didn't want to be here either. It let out a tiny hiss of resistance, but Chimera's imperious finger silenced its protests, and it shuffled on its belly across the sandy floor until it was lying in its own quarter circle, next to the earth zone where the mole was.

"Air!"

"Take me, take me!" The Nothing cried, jumping into the air as high as she could. "I have feathers! I can be useful!"

Chimera's concentration wavered.

"You're nothing," she hissed. "Go away before you ruin everything."

The Nothing sneezed and pooed on the floor, of course.

"Useless freak," Chimera snarled and swept The Nothing aside with a stroke of her wing. "Go and die some other place!"

"I'b so sorry," The Nothing whimpered, her tearful distress clogging her sinuses even worse than usual. "I'b tried. I really hab! But it's actually bery difficult *not* to live once you'b started!"

The Nothing flapped her wings frantically and managed to raise herself perhaps two or three feet above the sand in the cave, and so almost collided with a large grey bird that came sweeping in from the same direction as the seal. It wasn't a seagull, but a greylag goose, with a glossy scarlet beak and broad black bars across its chest and neck. It swerved to one side to avoid the collision and landed awkwardly with flapping wings on the smooth cave floor. It honked in protest, and I thought it sounded a little like a small car beeping its horn at a truck, but when Chimera held up her clawed hand and crooked it, the goose stopped squawking immediately. It slumped down on its chest as if its legs could no longer carry it, and the flapping wings grew still.

"Fire," Chimera commanded next.

This time it took longer for something to emerge from the darkness. But finally I could hear the scuffle of claws against the bedrock, and a small, portly, spiky lizard crawled reluctantly into the circle. I recognized it immediately – it was a fire lizard like the ones I'd met last autumn at the third part of my witch trial. Being a cave-dweller, it wasn't quite as out of place as the other three, but even so it wasn't comfortable – it would have preferred to return to the darkness, it felt unsafe and exposed in the daylight streaming through the cracks in the rock above us, and it was scared of Chimera, though it obeyed her.

Chimera bent over the mole and seized it with one taloned hand. So swiftly that my mind refused to take it in, she sliced a claw across its throat. The mole gasped as if struggling for air, but instead blood gushed out both through its mouth and through the gaping wound below, soaking its black fur. She dropped the small, bleeding body into the middle of its quarter, and then, with a single surge of her wings, landed right behind the seal.

"No!" I cried out, or at least I tried to; my vision was still swimming from the whack that had knocked me off my feet, and my voice sounded even smaller and feebler than usual. Chimera was going to kill those animals! That was what she meant by blood arts, she meant to use their blood, she meant to...

She meant to use my blood.

I didn't even know what she wanted to use it for, but right now I didn't care.

"*CAT*," I screamed, both out loud and inside my mind with all my strength. "*Now*."

That *now* contained a multitude of meanings it would have taken me several minutes to explain – that he had to come, that we would have to fight together harder than we'd ever fought before, that this was it, and that I was ready, that it was now or never.

He didn't come. It was exactly like the time with the wild dogs, I called for help, but he didn't come, he'd abandoned me, he'd...

It was exactly like the time with the wild dogs.

Everything inside my mind went very quiet, like a film playing in slow motion with no sound. Yet again I watched as the jaws of Lop-Ear closed around my chin and my throat, I saw her teeth slip, pierce my skin, felt the blood move from me to her. My blood. The blood of Viridian.

"Remember Viridian," I whispered.

CHAPTER 24

Life Stealer

*B*lessed Powers. *The girl is still wet behind the ears. And completely untrained!*

I looked down at my body and it was like seeing myself through the eyes of a stranger. Eyes that viewed me as a child, unfinished and weak, almost as useless as The Nothing.

She hasn't even grown breasts yet!

I wouldn't have thought it possible to blush and get embarrassed while I was in mortal danger, but I did. I instinctively raised my arms and folded them across my chest.

Stand up, girl! The new, bossy voice in my head ordered me. *Up-up-up!*

Suddenly I was back on my feet. Chimera, who had been bending over the seal in the wheel's water zone, straightened up immediately. She half-turned and stretched one wing in my direction, probably to knock me to the ground again.

Revulsion surged in me like a black wave.

Blood thief, the voice inside me hissed. *Life stealer!*

"Let go of that which is not yours!" The voice that came out of my mouth was deeper than my own, hard and alien. And then it happened... I don't know how... it's so difficult to...

I can't explain it. Something came out of me. Something sharp and shiny, like a knife or a sword. Yes, like a sword. There was even a singing, metallic sound in the air.

And Chimera screamed.

One of her wings lay on the ground. It kept its shape for a brief moment, then it began to dissolve in front of my very eyes. It disintegrated feather by feather, and each feather shimmered and became a bird. A thrush, a sparrow, a buzzard, a heron. A giant white-tailed sea eagle, a tiny wren.

There were hundreds of them. Not living birds, even I could see that, completely untrained and still wet behind the ears though I was. There was something pale and transparent about them, and the wing of the eagle went right through the thrush, without either of them noticing it. Ghost birds. Or more accurately perhaps, bird spirits. They were all that remained of the living animals whose life and... and *birdness* Chimera had claimed – a life for every single feather. *That* was the price of Chimera's wings.

"And the other one," I whispered to the new voice inside me.

Chimera was reeling; she was being dragged down by the weight of her remaining wing now that the severed one was no longer there to counterbalance it.

I don't think I'd even needed to ask. The sword-like feeling welled up in me before the words had even left my lips. It hurt this time, more than the first. As if the sword had to cut its way out of me before we could liberate the stolen lives trapped in Chimera's other wing. But the second wing fell too. And the cave was filled with the rush and call of birds, with hoarse caws and honks and tweets, with the squawking of gulls and the cries of buzzards, bewildered but free. In a roar of invisible wings, they rose and soared and finally disappeared as if the walls of the cave had ceased to exist.

Chimera's eyes had taken on a maddened gleam. Now it was her turn to curl up in the sand of the cave, without a feather on her body. Even her talons had shrunk to very long nails.

"Mum!" The Nothing squawked, huddling against her legs. "What's happening?"

Chimera kicked her so violently that the little bundle of feathers hurtled through the air and crashed into the wall of the cave with an ugly, wet smack.

"No!" I screamed, somehow more outraged at this one, hopeless life than the hundreds of others that hadn't sneezed and pooed on me, or asked me what the word "friend" meant. "Don't you dare! **GO AWAY! Go! Vanish. Get out of my life and STAY OUT. I want you GONE for GOOD!**"

The words came from deep, deep inside me. They were as sharp as the invisible sword had been. They burst out of me, sticky with blood and scorching heat, and hit Chimera like a hammer blow.

If she had screamed when the voice helped me take her first wing, it was nothing compared to what she did now. Her scream seemed to absorb all the air in the cave, so that for a very long moment I couldn't even breathe. It went on and on. There was as much bird in that cry as there was a human voice, there was mortal fear and pain, but also hatred, rage and a thirst for revenge.

Youuuuu...

Willllllllllll...

Payyyyyyyyyyyyyyy...

Forrrrrrrrrrrrrrrr...

Thissssssssssssss....

I covered my ears with my hands, but it wasn't enough. I had to close my eyes too.

Not until it had been quiet for a while did I open my eyes again. She was gone. She had vanished completely, as I'd ordered her to. Not so much as a feather or a strand of hair was left behind.

Blessed Powers, the voice inside me murmured. *The girl is a proper witch after all...*

The four animals inside the wheel were still there. The seal, the wild goose and the fire lizard all peered up at me uncertainly, as if they couldn't quite believe that it was over. The mole looked at nothing, saw nothing. A final tremor went through its dark little body, then it was gone.

"Go," I said to the others. "You're free. Go now..."

The word "free" made me think of The Nothing, and I turned away from the circle without worrying about what happened to the three living animals.

She was lying on the floor under the outcrop she had smashed into, a forlorn little figure never much suited to life. Even so, I found it hard to bear that she had died without ever knowing what words such as freedom, friendship and happiness really meant. I knelt down beside her and gently touched her damp, filthy feathers. She was still warm; the heat of life doesn't leave a body as quickly as that. But... surely that was... Yes. It was there, a faint breath, a fragile and stumbling heartbeat. She was still alive.

"Save her," I pleaded, because I didn't know how to do it myself, and I had a feeling that this new but ancient voice inside me was wiser than me in this respect, too.

Are you sure that's what she wants?

I had to think about this before I replied. Life was hard for The Nothing. The way she was created, the way Chimera had created her, there wasn't a lot she could do for herself.

"Can't we help?" I said softly. "Give her... some decent legs, perhaps. Or a pair of wings she can actually use for flying."

Whose life will you take to give them to her? the voice asked with glacial chill. *And have you even asked her if that is what she wants?*

It felt as if I'd been slapped across my face, only on the inside. Very uncomfortable. But then it dawned on me that if I started changing The Nothing without her consent, I was no better than Chimera.

"Chimera didn't care whether The Nothing lived or died," I said in my own defence. "I do."

And what does the poor creature herself want?

"She said that it was hard not to go on living once you had started," I said. "And perhaps... perhaps there might be time for her to learn the meaning of freedom. And friendship."

My hands started moving without my direction. They placed themselves gently on The Nothing's damp, feathered chest, one on top of the other. And suddenly I began singing. A wordless hum, simultaneously high and low, as if I was singing two notes at the same time. My head was buzzing and spinning, and I paused for a moment when I realized that what was coming out of me was wildsong, wildsong like Aunt Isa's.

Stop resisting, child! the voice said irritably. *We're both exhausted, and it's hard enough as it is.*

There were so many questions I wanted answered. What was happening to me? Whose was that old, bossy voice, and what was she doing in my head? Could I get rid of her again? And if I could – would I want to?

But those questions would have to wait if I were to save The Nothing. If *we* were to save The Nothing. Because I couldn't do it alone.

I closed my eyes and let the wildsong come as it might.

CHAPTER 25

Something Is Better Than Nothing

The cave had grown both cold and dark when I came round again. Yet I felt, at least for the brief moment that passed before I woke up properly, both warm and safe.

I wasn't alone. Along my back lay a familiar lithe and furry body, and next to my tummy, a curled-up feathered figure the size of a football, limp and unmoving, but warm and alive. Cat and The Nothing.

I hadn't passed out or anything equally dramatic. I'd simply fallen asleep. When the wildsong had finished with me and The Nothing, I had been so exhausted that I had to lie down for a moment. That moment had apparently turned into several hours, according to my watch.

I had to get out of here. But how? I didn't seriously believe that I could cast a spell and whizz myself back to the drawing room at Westmark, in the same way that had brought me here, nor did I have any desire to try.

The voice inside my head didn't offer any helpful suggestions either. In fact, it was rather quiet in there.

"Hello?" I said tentatively. "Is anyone here?"

It wasn't until I said it out loud, that I realized how truly crazy it was to try to have a conversation with... with... with...

With Viridian. Because suddenly I knew with absolute certainty who it was I had summoned, knew whose voice had spoken inside me – regardless of how that had come about.

"Viridian." I only whispered the name, it felt way too risky to say it out loud.

Cat stretched out and dug his claws into my neck – not hard enough to pierce my skin, just a Cat warning.

I'm here, he said, with a slight emphasis on *I'm*. As far as he was concerned, that had to be enough – how could I possibly need anyone else?

"Cat? Can we use the wildways to get out of here?"

It took a while before he replied.

Better not to, he then said. *Too close to the wheel. Better not risk... waking anything up.*

A shiver went down my spine when he said it, and it put a stop to my feeling warm and safe.

"We need to get out," I said. "As quickly as possible."

There had to be a way out. Chimera might be able to magic herself in and out of here, but the goose and the seal couldn't have. They'd both arrived using more traditional methods. Now I was somewhat bigger than the goose, but... what was it Viridian had written in her book: "There was only one way out and that was to follow the trickle of the wellspring, through the passage it had carved to reach the sea."

The wellspring was still here somewhere. I could hear it.

It took me at least a scrambling, creeping and climbing hour to follow the spring and its passage through caves and caverns down to the shoreline below Westmark. I was tired, it was pitch black in the caverns, and I was carrying The Nothing. I'd made a kind of pouch for her by folding up the hem of my T-shirt and tying a knot in it, and she didn't weigh very much – next to nothing in fact – but I had to hold her with one hand all the time so she didn't fall out.

It was a cold and frost-clear night, and the moon was almost full. It lit up the shore like a blue spotlight. Mounds of seaweed glistened with blue hoar frost, the crusty ice on the puddles had turned blue and even Cat's fur took on a blueish sheen.

We had escaped. However, now that the cave no longer shielded us against the cold, I soon began to tremble so badly I could barely walk. And when I saw how steep the cliffs were, I was sorely tempted to just sit down and have a good cry. I was so tired, tired in my body, tired in my head, but most of all tired and sore inside, in that place where the invisible sword had sprung from.

"I know you always say I should never give up before I've fought," I whispered feebly to Cat. "But how about afterwards?"

Just then I heard a soft cry above us, and a broad shadow on silent wings swooped closely over my head. I ducked instinctively, but this time it wasn't a shark bird or a soul-stripped seagull. It was Hoot-Hoot.

"There they are," a familiar voice called out from behind me. "I can see them!"

And when I turned around, I saw Oscar come running across the blue sand, waving his arms and making a small leap of joy every now and then.

"Here they are, here they are, here they are..."

He came to an abrupt halt right in front of me. I could see that he wanted to give me a hug, but we don't touch each other so much these days because the others will just tease us even more about snogging (and we really don't!) But right now school was very far away. I didn't give a monkey's about anyone from our class. I didn't even care about Alex and his moronic remarks about witches and magic. Except that...

"Oscar?"

"Yes?"

"Are you going to tell Alex about this as well?"

He pulled a face.

"I told him not to tell anyone else," he mumbled. "It was just that... I just think it's so cool..." He looked up at me, and for once his cheeky face was deadly serious. "I'm so sorry," he said. "I shouldn't have told him."

"No. You shouldn't have. And if you tell anyone about what I'm about to do, then... then I really will get Aunt Isa to turn you into a frog!"

He actually looked a tad alarmed. "She wouldn't do that," he said. "Would she...? And what... what exactly are you going to do?"

"Oh, just shut up."

I put my arms around him and hugged him until I heard a small, sleepy "ouch" from The Nothing. We both started laughing. And then we had to hug each other again, but more gently this time.

"We've been looking for you for hours," Oscar said. "Isa said you were near the shore, but we still couldn't find you."

"No," I said. "There was a cave. An... an underground cave. It... it was hard to find the way out." Suddenly I became aware of how much my legs were shaking underneath me, and I had to slide down on my haunches so as not to fall.

"Are you OK?" he said with a worried look.

"I don't know," I said, tentatively, because a multitude of things were whirling around inside my head. Viridian's voice was silent now, but I could still remember what it was like to see myself through her eyes and find a small, ignorant, untrained child. Not nice. And I had a terrifying sensation of bleeding on the inside, not in my stomach or my lungs or anything like that, but in that place in me where wildsense and blood art and everything else came from. I might not be bleeding profusely from a stab wound or shark bird's bite, yet I had been wounded. I didn't know how to heal that kind of injury, but Aunt Isa might.

I couldn't explain any of that to Oscar, at least not right now. I said something simpler, easier.

"I'm freezing. I can't even feel my legs."

"Come with me," Oscar said. "There's a way up with steps and so on further along. And I think that Shanaia's got a fire going up at the house."

Cat stretched, yawned and swatted me with a broad paw. *So what are we waiting for?*

They'd left the drawing room – I imagined that all three of them had had more than enough of it – and were warming up in front of a tall, white stove in what Shanaia called the garden room, though it was clearly more room than garden. The only flowers were those on the wallpaper. Suddenly I could see that this had to be the home of a wildwitch. There were pictures of animals and birds on the walls, books about animals and birds on the bookshelves, dusty jars and pots of desiccated herbs, nesting boxes and dog baskets – Woofer had already picked the comfiest one – and cardboard boxes lined with cotton wool and newspaper, just like the hedgehog boxes back at Aunt Isa's.

"Here," Aunt Isa said, handing me a steaming cup of some kind of witch's brew. "Drink it as hot as you can without scalding yourself."

I sat wrapped in three blankets with my legs tucked up underneath me on a bamboo sofa with faded, floral cushions. The Nothing was still asleep on my tummy, but would snore and sneeze occasionally. I told them what had happened in the cave as best I could, but I struggled to explain many things properly. For example, how Chimera had lost her wings.

"You cut them off her?" Oscar asked, confused. "How? With a knife? Wasn't there a lot of blood?"

"Not with a knife," I said. "It was more like... it came from in here..." I pointed to the lower part of my ribs. "I don't really..."

"Magic?" he said eagerly. "Did you use magic?"

"Yes... I... suppose I did." But that didn't ring true either. Magic was all about waving wands and fire balls and magic spells. I'd never heard of magic that cut its way out of your chest and weirdly made you bleed on the inside.

I could feel Aunt Isa's eyes on me, but I kept staring into my teacup.

"Clara. I'm sorry," she said. "I should have known better than... than to resort to blood arts."

"Blood arts?" Oscar's ears pricked up. "What's that?"

"What I was trying to do with the wheel. Earth, water, air and fire, and blood, which binds it all together because blood is earth, water, air and fire. I had a hunch that was how the oblivion curse had been created in the first place, so it was what I thought I needed to do in order to lift it. But instead..."

She threw up her hands. "Blood has a will of its own. Blood wants blood, the saying goes, and that's why blood arts can be difficult to control. And worse – blood arts require a very pure heart or it becomes murder. I... I shouldn't have run that risk with you, and definitely not without you understanding what you were agreeing to."

"If you hadn't done it, we might still be up in that drawing room. Or worse," I said. "What happened to the shark birds?"

"It was insane," Oscar said. "They just started dropping out of the sky. We could see them through the window and hear them crash onto the floor in the hall. Some of them... some turned into ordinary, living birds and flew away. But most of them ended up as strange little heaps of feathers, bones and teeth. Totally Halloween-like. Zombie birds!"

I thought about the feathers in Chimera's wings. One life for each feather. *Blood arts require a very pure heart or it becomes murder.* Life stealer, Viridian had called Chimera.

"Were they created using blood art?" I asked Aunt Isa.

"Yes."

"Gross," Oscar said.

"I don't want to turn into someone like that," I said, and finally looked up at Aunt Isa. "I really don't."

"Clara! I assure you, you won't!"

But I had my doubts. There was something about my blood. Viridian's blood. My blood lives on in my heirs, Viridian had written in her book. And somehow, across four centuries, she had passed it on to me.

It wasn't a nice feeling.

The Nothing could hardly believe it.

"You *want* me to come with you?" she said over and over. "With *you*? You don't *mind*?"

"Yes," said Aunt Isa. "If you'd like to you can live with me. Perhaps you can help me sort out my papers. After all, you know how to read and write, don't you?"

"Yes," The Nothing said, startled. "I..."

"Then that's a deal. That is, if you'd like to?"

The Nothing sneezed. The tears were still rolling down her cheeks, but her eyes were happy.

"I'd like that very much," she said and looked as if she had been given ten years' worth of birthday presents all at once.

Shanaia, however, didn't want to come home with us.

"I *am* home," she said. "I'm not leaving Westmark again!"

"You're not strong enough to live on your own for the time being," Aunt Isa protested. "You're not well enough. Please come with us – I promise I'll help you get back here when you're better."

Shanaia just shook her head. "I'm staying where I am," she declared.

Aunt Isa didn't like it, I could tell from looking at her. But she also knew that both my mum and Oscar's were going out of their minds with worry.

"I'll come back to see you soon," Aunt Isa said. "As soon as I can."

A pale Shanaia nodded.

"You don't have to be so nice to me," she said. "I know exactly what I did."

"If we can forgive you," Aunt Isa said, "then don't you think you might consider forgiving yourself?"

Shanaia just looked down and whispered something I couldn't hear.

"What did you say?" Aunt Isa asked her.

"I just said yes."

But I was pretty sure she hadn't. She was far from ready for easy excuses and quick forgiveness.

We left her there, on the stone steps outside the main entrance to Westmark, but none of us liked to see her so alone.

"If only she could find herself a new wildfriend," Aunt Isa said. "She definitely hasn't recovered from the death of Elfrida yet."

The moment she said it, the kestrel took off from the weathervane up on the roof and came swooping in a sharp arc over our heads towards Shanaia. Startled, she held out her arm and the kestrel landed on her wrist. I couldn't help smiling.

"I think that's being taken care of," I said softly.

CHAPTER 26

Excuses

"Woofer ran away and I had to find him," Oscar told the police officer.

We hadn't even discussed what to say when we came back. To be honest, I don't think any of us had thought that far ahead, not even Aunt Isa. She was clearly much better at fixing broken bird wings and healing fevers than inventing convincing excuses for mums and police officers.

Oscar's excuse was a good cover story because it was simple, easy to remember and even true – in parts. Nevertheless, some aspects stretched credibility.

"For over forty-eight hours?" the officer said with raised eyebrows. "And at no point were you able to phone home or contact an adult?"

"Eh... I was... ahem... out of reach," Oscar said, pulling down his sleeves to conceal the shark bird bites. "I mean, my phone had gone dead. No battery. No coverage. Both, in fact!"

The officer looked hard at Oscar. Then at Oscar's mum. And then back at Oscar. He clearly suspected Oscar of having run away from home to get into the kind of trouble teenage boys shouldn't get into. Glue sniffing, joyriding or live action role-playing. Something along those lines.

"And you, young lady? What have you got to say for yourself?"

The young lady was me. I stared at the toes of my wellies and cleared my throat a couple of times.

"Nothing," I said. "Or that is... I was just helping him. To find Woofer."

The police officer heaved an exasperated sigh and snapped shut his notebook.

"Very well," he said. "Seeing as you're both home safe and sound. And no crime appears to have been committed. But don't let it happen again. Do you understand?"

We both nodded so vehemently it must have looked as if our heads were about to fall off.

The officer said goodbye to Oscar's mum, scowled at Woofer, whom he clearly felt ought to be held partly responsible for the upheaval, and trudged down the stairs muttering into his radio. That was the police dealt with, I thought. Now only Oscar's mum was left... and mine.

We'd gone to Oscar's first because he'd been gone

the longest. I texted my mum so she knew that I was all right and on my way home. But even so, I was dreading what she had to say.

Nor did Oscar look as if he fancied a one-on-one with his mum. It was glaringly obvious that she wouldn't be fobbed off with the "I had to find Woofer" story.

Her face was very tight, as if she was making a great effort not to start screaming and shouting and throwing furniture about.

"You. Home. Now," she ordered me. Then she pointed at Oscar with an unbelievably sharp index finger. "You, into the shower. And afterwards, I expect to get a very good explanation."

As I made my way to my own front door, I wondered what he would say. The truth was so... implausible. His mum didn't have a sister who was a wildwitch. The wildest thing anyone in her family ever got up to was probably a trip to the zoo. If he tried to explain what had really happened – wildways, shark birds, blood arts and the whole shebang – she would undoubtedly conclude that he was lying. Or had lost his marbles. But what else could he say?

Perhaps I was lucky in that my mum would actually believe me.

"Hi," I called out from the hall.

There was no reply, though the light was on and I could hear the muffled sound of some news channel on the television.

My mum was sitting at one end of the sofa. At the other end was my dad. He pressed the remote control and turned off the television when I walked in.

"Where have you been?" he asked. "Clara, what on earth happened?"

I just stood there with my mouth hanging open, not knowing what to say. I hadn't thought about my dad for a second. I was so used to him not being around, or rather, I'd filed him in a box labelled Chestnut Street and Holiday Dad. It hadn't even crossed my mind to wonder what I would say to *him*.

I sent my mum a desperate, sideways glance. Had she told him anything about Aunt Isa and the wildworld while I'd been gone? Or was my dad still as ignorant as Oscar's mum?

"Oscar's dog ran away..." I began pathetically.

"You left a note," Mum said, and her voice was trembling. "Clara, you left a note, and then you disappeared." She took a deep breath. "Try to imagine for one moment that I had done the same to you. That I had slipped out of the flat one evening and just left a note telling you not to worry. And then *stayed* away for thirty-six hours without even a text message. How do you think you would have felt?"

But mums don't do that, I thought instantly and I nearly blurted it out loud.

"My phone wasn't working," I tried.

"Were you with Isa?" Mum wanted to know. "Was that where you were? Is this her fault?"

"No... or I mean, yes, in a way. Aunt Isa was there too..."

My dad looked from one to the other as if he were watching a tennis match. He frowned.

"What's all this about Isa?" he said. "I didn't think the two of you were that close?"

I could tell he was reassured that at least another adult had been involved.

"Aunt Isa has helped us a lot," I said. "Mum, you remember. Last autumn, when I was ill... if it hadn't been for Aunt Isa..."

I could see Mum battling with herself. If wishing could make it so, I think she would have made Aunt Isa and all the wildworld disappear in one big puff of smoke. There had been times, mostly last year, when I would have done the same. But now I wouldn't want to be without Aunt Isa. And Cat. And Bumble and Star and The Nothing, and the kestrel and Lop-Ear and...

In fact, I didn't want to be without any of it. Well, possibly Chimera. I could have done without her.

"I like Aunt Isa," I said firmly.

"Well, that's a good thing," Dad said, somewhat confused. I think he could tell that there was more going on than he knew about. "Perhaps I ought to meet your Aunt Isa soon. So I can find out a little more about what you... experience... when you're with her."

"Isa lives quite a different life from ours," my mum said.

"How do you mean?" he asked.

"Well, she lives... deep in the countryside. More like... in tune with nature."

"So what?" my dad said. "Where's the harm in our daughter learning that life can be lived in more than one way?"

I watched Mum fight the temptation to explain to him exactly what made Aunt Isa so different, but I also knew that she wouldn't do it. Not after devoting years of her life to making us look like ordinary, normal, non-witchy people, and for just as many years had concealed the fact that she had a sister who could only be described as a witch. It wasn't a secret she intended to reveal now.

"I'm sorry if I made you worry, Dad," I said, hugging him. "I didn't mean to."

"Yes, yes, Munchkin," he said, kissing my hair somewhere above my right ear. "Just don't let it happen again. Promise?"

The discussion didn't finish there. I could hear them talking quietly in the living room when they thought I'd fallen asleep. Dad simply couldn't understand why Mum was so opposed to Aunt Isa.

"So is it because she's completely irresponsible?"

"No," Mum said. "That would be unfair. Just very... alternative."

"Earth toilets and wickerwork?"

"Something like that."

"Clara likes her, and it sounds as if she benefits from being with her."

"You don't get it. I know my sister better than you do. You don't understand..."

"No, so you keep saying. But I understand this much: I think it would be a huge mistake for you to ban Clara from seeing her own aunt. Give her your blessing. That'll put an end to the panic and the disappearing acts and heart-breaking little notes."

Mum said nothing. She was silent for a long time. I yawned, turned over and could feel sleep getting ever more tempting. But whenever I closed my eyes everything would go dark red, and red shadows with sharp claws and teeth would close in on me.

"Cat?" I whispered into the darkness. "Cat, please would you come and... be with me for a little while?"

"What if I were to tell you..." It was my mum's voice from the living room, a little too loud and strained. "What if I were to tell you that what Clara does with Isa is dangerous?"

"Dangerous. How?"

"Just... dangerous."

"Mind-altering drugs? Wild car chases? Juvenile delinquency?"

"No, no. Nothing like that."

"Then what are you so afraid of?"

"That... that Clara will change. That she might have some kind of accident. That..." Mum took a deep breath. "That she'll turn into someone else."

"Milla. She's not a little girl any more. Growing up is always dangerous. But it's necessary."

Suddenly I could feel something warm against my back. Cat was purring so much that my whole body was humming.

Sleep, he said. *I'll look out for you. For a little while longer.*

I never heard what my mum said, or if she even replied at all. Nor did I manage to ask Cat what he meant by "a little while longer". I fell asleep, and if I had any dreams, I'd forgotten them by the next morning.

CHAPTER 27

Cat Smiles

It felt totally insane to get up to go to school the next day. I'd expected it to feel normal. After all, it was what I did most mornings, but somehow normality and witchery had traded places. These days it seemed quite reasonable and normal to wonder if The Nothing would enjoy living with Aunt Isa, and if more of Viridian's words would appear in the books of Westmark, now that the oblivion curse had been lifted. Instead, I couldn't even remember what day it was and what my first lesson would be, and even if I'd been able to, it felt completely pointless and irrelevant.

"Are you tired, Mouse?" Mum asked when she pulled up outside the school gate. We were late – much too late – so there wasn't the usual traffic jam.

"A little," I said.

"Perhaps you should have stayed at home after all." She let go of the gearstick and rested her hand against my cheek for a moment. "I don't want you getting ill again."

"Again?"

"Yes. Like last autumn."

"But I won't." And yet I couldn't help touching the claw marks on my forehead. I knew now that the business with the claws, the blood and Cat Scratch Disease had been necessary so that Cat and I could communicate, but that didn't mean it hadn't seemed terrifying and dangerous back when I had no idea what was going on. "Mum, it was only so that Cat..."

"Yes, yes, Clara Mouse," she said quickly, as if she would rather not talk about it. "But promise me you'll take care of yourself and come straight home from school, won't you? Particularly if you start feeling ill."

"I won't get ill again," I said. "But... OK." After all, she was only trying to take care of me. Except that we'd both started realizing how many things in the world she couldn't protect me from. I gave her a quick peck on the cheek, very much not my usual bah-I-have-to-go-to-school way of saying goodbye to her. Then I jumped out of the car, and waved as she drove off.

I was looking at the car and so didn't notice that I wasn't the only kid to turn up five minutes after the bell had gone. However, one of the stragglers had noticed me.

"Watch where you're going, loser," said Martin the Meanie from Year 10, though I wasn't about to bump into him this time; then he punched my shoulder and positioned himself right in the middle of the school gate. He looked a bit like a goalkeeper who wasn't going to let the ball get past him. With me being the ball.

"Right," he said. "Are you going to apologize then?"

"What for?" I said.

"For being a pathetic loser who's always in my way. That's what for."

His eyes were tiny, glittering cracks. He had a red, angry scratch on one cheek, near his ear, and his hand also looked bruised and swollen. Had he been in a fight? Few boys at school would dare to pick a fight with him, but then again, there was a world outside the school gates.

I sized him up. He hadn't grown any shorter. But then, he didn't have sharp, triangular fangs either, nor metre-high wings created from stolen bird lives, and it was quite remarkable how harmless that suddenly made him look.

"I'm sorry, but I really haven't got time for this," I said abruptly and marched straight past him.

I think he was too shocked to react. Or perhaps there was just enough wildwitch in me to stop him. At any rate, he didn't touch me.

Cat strolled along by my side. He hadn't been there a moment ago, but he was here now.

If you want me to claw him, I will.

I looked down and met his yellow cat's eyes. I wasn't sure that I'd forgiven him yet for leaving me in the lurch with the wild dogs *and* Chimera.

"Why are you being so helpful all of a sudden?" I said sourly.

He just looked at me and flashed me a bright white-fanged cat smile.

I shook my head. "Thanks, but no thanks. I've got this one."

His cat smile broadened. Smugness radiated from him like heat off a radiator. I had a strong feeling that I'd finally passed a test he felt I ought to pass. He purred loudly.

That's why, he said, and disappeared in a cloud of wildways fog.

Have I mentioned that Cat usually gets the last word?

NEXT IN THE WILDWITCH SERIES

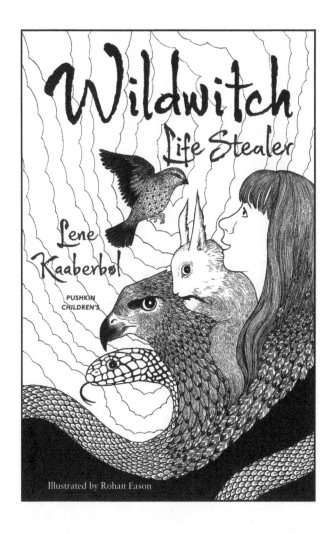

PUSHKIN CHILDREN'S BOOKS

Just as we all are, children are fascinated by stories. From the earliest age, we love to hear about monsters and heroes, romance and death, disaster and rescue, from every place and time.

We created Pushkin Children's Books to share these tales from different languages and cultures with younger readers, and to open the door to the wide, colourful worlds these stories offer.

From picture books and adventure stories to fairy tales and classics, and from fifty-year-old bestsellers to current huge successes abroad, the books on the Pushkin Children's list reflect the very best stories from around the world, for our most discerning readers of all: children.